Jar of Hearts

By: Sayword B. Eller

Other books by Sayword B. Eller

Second Chances; and other tales of love

Available at www.lulu.com

Published by At Fault Publishing

First printing 2012

To Miranda, Stephanie, and Ares.
Thank you for being my biggest fans.
I love you.

And to my husband. Je t'aime.

Table of Contents

* Story was originally featured on prompting365.com
1 writer, 1 daily prompt, 365 days.

Redemption

(a sequel to Promises)

I.

"Dakota, hun, you are going to be fine." I paused, waiting for my overly-paranoid friend to gush another mouthful of hardly-interpretable words through the other end of the phone. It was hard not to laugh when they were finally understandable. "Will you just chill! This is not your first pregnancy. I am almost there."

When the house came into sight I closed the phone, knowing all too well that she had worked herself into too much of a frenzy to realize I wasn't there until the door opened.

True to form she was still seated on her brown battered sofa, one hand rubbing her bulging belly, sobbing into the receiver.

"I'm here!" I attempted over her hysterics. "Here is your sandwich." I dropped the bag in her lap, removing the phone from her hand. "And your favorite milkshake!"

The tears were gone the moment the bag opened. "Thank you, Janey," she said, sniffling as she bit into the provolone and swiss on rye.

"No problem. Now, tell me what's up." I sat on the table in front of her, our knees touching. "I can't keep leaving the store every time you're having a meltdown."

"I know," she moaned. "I just feel so… *alone!*"

I stifled a laugh. This second pregnancy was certainly more dramatic than her first had been almost eleven years ago. Of course then Dakota had been twenty-four and oblivious to anything other than the euphoria of love from her new relationship and the bundle on the way. Now she was mid-thirties and the euphoria of love had gone long ago. Now it was a comfortable love, one filled with the knowledge that she would always have someone in her corner. It was something I wish I had been able to have with John. Now days he was busy in his own euphoric haze. His new girlfriend was nice enough. More than once I have found myself thanking my lucky stars that we never had children. I don't think I could handle another woman playing mommy to my child.

"You're not alone, sweetie," I said. "You've got Daniel and Danny."

She huffed. "Daniel is too busy with everybody else and Danny hates me cause I'm having another baby."

"And you've always got me." I tried to force her to look at me. To hear what I was saying to her, but she just kept staring at that damn sandwich. When the tears began to spill down her cheeks again, I stood up. I don't know why I get frustrated at times like these. I know it's counter-productive. "Come on."

She looked up, seemingly surprised by my change in tone. "What? Are you mad at me too?"

I laughed. "No, I'm not mad at you. We're getting you out of this house. You're going to the store with me."

She shook her head. "I can't. Danny will be home..."

"Later," I finished, pointing to the digital clock on her cable box. "Look, it's only eleven thirty. The kid won't be home until after four. You've got time! I'll bring you back at three-thirty."

"I've got laundry and dishes," she tried, but I could see her resolve fading. She wanted out as much as I wanted to get her out.

"They will keep. Now get off your duff and let's go!"

By the time we got in the car it was almost noon, and by the time we got to my quaint little store it was a quarter after. I hadn't been at this location long, only about two years, but it had proven to be a great spot and most days, when I actually opened and could stay in the store, it was just profitable enough to sustain me. Of course I had come out pretty good after my divorce, with John offering to pay alimony and me not denying it. Sure I felt bad, especially since it had been mostly my idea to split up, but money speaks louder than guilt for some people and I am definitely one of those. So, with my alimony and my little bit of profit I manage to pay the bills for my building and the apartment above.

"Didn't think you was coming in today," Ruby, one of my regulars, quipped when Dakota and I finally reached the double doors to my Rags and Bones Thrift and consignment.

"It was my fault, Ruby," Dakota said, rubbing her belly. I had noticed more than once that the belly was brought into situations where Dakota might not have fared very well usually. "I was feeling pretty bad."

Ruby wasn't buying. "Well, ain't you got a husband?"

I turned the key in the brass lock and pushed open the door, ushering my best friend inside. "Okay, Ruby, watch it," I said with a chuckle. "The door's open, go ahead and shop."

"Can you believe what she just said to me?" Dakota huffed as I pushed her along to the desk on the left.

"She's Ruby, of course I can believe it. You just need to remind yourself that she's a million years old and hates everybody."

Dakota laughed.

"Now, put your feet up and try out the new television I found over the weekend."

"Another junk find, huh?"

I turned my head to the side. "Another man's junk is…"

"Yeah, yeah, yeah." She dropped down on the old green rocking chair that had hosted many bottoms since its creation in 1974.

As she settled in to watch The Jeffersons, her favorite, I made my way into the back room, grabbing the closest box and carrying it out onto the floor.

"Janey, why'd you bring that girl in here?" Ruby asked, sidling up beside me as I priced and tossed up a few dozen stuffed Chihuahuas from the Taco Bell campaign of the late 90s.

"Now what on earth do you mean, Ruby?"

"How you gonna find a man if you've got knocked up Nessy in here?"

"First of all," I said, looking back to make sure that Dakota was still watching George and Weezy. "I am not the pregnant one. Secondly, I am not looking for a man right now."

"Humph" was her only reply.

There had been dates since the dissolution of my marriage, but no one that had managed to capture my heart. I know what you're thinking. Sure the name Ryan creeps into my mind sometimes, but then the name Kim follows it and I push it away. I've seen him once or twice, in fact, but only from a distance and I never made myself known. No, I wasn't pulling the stalker girl thing. Not anymore.

"Excuse me," a voice said from behind us.

I turned, my standard *how may I help you* smile pasted across my face. She was twenty-six-ish and blond with a pretty heart-shaped mouth and high cheekbones. Her hair curled around her jaw bouncing every time her head moved as if saying *hi!* "Yes?"

"That woman over there said you were the owner of this…" A curious look slid over her face, then after a moment it was gone and she was smiling again. "Forgive me," she said. "You just look so familiar. Have we met?"

"I don't think so." and I really didn't. "I am the owner. Perhaps you've been in before."

"No, this is my first time."

"Oh. Well, how can I help you?"

She still looked as though she wanted to continue the *where have I seen you game*, but she turned pointing to the front window. "You've got a baby carriage up there that I think my sister would love."

"Oh? Is she expecting?"

"Uh-huh. It's her second one. She and her husband got married, like four or five years ago. My niece turned three a few months ago. They told everyone about this baby on Ginny's birthday."

"Ginny? How cute." We were walking toward the front window, me trying desperately not to let my size sixteen hips bump into the bits and pieces sticking out along the way. Of course little miss size zero didn't have a problem at all. I suddenly found myself hating her sister, assuming that she shared the same stick-figure gene.

"Yeah, her name is Genevieve, but we all just call her Ginny."

Her perkiness was beyond annoying.

I pulled the tag off of the prize of my little shop and turned, tugging the vintage oversized man shirt I had chosen to wear on the one day a teeny tiny beauty queen happened into my shop, down over my curves.

"It's early twentieth century, wicker, and is in exceptional condition. There is a nice pillow inside and the handle can be adjusted so that the baby faces front or toward its parents."

"It's just precious!" she squealed and I moved aside for her to run those perfectly manicured hands over the bright white wicker.

It had taken hours with a toothbrush to expose the beauty this tween was gushing over. Okay, so I know a tween is a pre-teen, but at that moment I wasn't the biggest fan of skinny girls.

"Yes, it is."

"How much?"

This is normally where I lost people. "Two hundred."

"Really?"

"Yes."

Her blue eyes fell back to the carriage. "It's nice... Two hundred, really?"

"Yes." I turned to put the little white string back around the porcelain-clad handle. "That's actually a fair price for a piece like this," I added.

"I found it!" she squealed.

I turned around to find that her pink blackberry was pressed up against the side of her head.

"Yeah, at this cute little place downtown. It's a..." She covered the phone. "What years did you say?" she asked me.

"Early twentieth," I supplied.

"Early twentieth century. Uh-huh. Uh-huh. So you'll pick it up and take it to my house? Great!" Without saying goodbye she pressed end and shoved the little phone into her Dolce and Gabbana (probably a knockoff) bag. "I'll take it!"

"Wow, what kind of drugs is she on?" Dakota asked as blondie bounced across the refurbished hardwood floors and out the door.

"Who knows. Her sister is preggers, though," I turned to her, poking her belly. "Just like you." A smile spread across her face. "I wanted to get that carriage for you."

"It would have just got broken."

I slid my arm around my friend and sighed. "I bet that little shit has a really hot boyfriend and they have great skinny sex."

Dakota laughed. "You could have skinny sex too if you would get over yourself and go out with some of these guys that are asking you."

"Blah, blah, blah. Can you believe that chick was here for so long! What did Ruby buy?"

"Some old magazines and a busted up lamp. Why didn't she take the carriage with her? It's not like it weighs a ton."

"Apparently she was just on lunch. She's sending someone to pick it up." I held up the tag. "They've even got to tell me a password."

Dakota laughed. "Ah, covert operation, huh?"

"I guess. Come on, I've got to get you home and get back here before this tag explodes."

It was ten past three when I opened the doors to my shop again. Monday afternoons were quiet, and today was no exception. As four o'clock rolled around I watched the streaks of yellow as the big buses began their treks to take the little children home to their mommies and daddies.

At half past the phone rang, "Rags N Bones thrift and consignment," I answered.

"Janey."

"John."

"What time do you close up shop?"

"Six o'clock, as usual. Why?"

"I need to see you."

Consider my interest peaked. "Me? Why?"

"I just do, okay?"

"Okay. How's Evie?" Why I asked is beyond me.

"Huh? Oh, she's fine. Look, I'll be by in a little while."

He showed up sooner than that. I hadn't seen my ex-husband look so bad since the day we decided it would be best to just part ways. I kind of thought that he hated me on that day, but during the divorce he had assured me that it wasn't quite hate, only dislike.

When the door chimed at five o'clock I expected it to be the carriage guy, but there was my ex-husband looking exhausted and lost, his dark hair blown this way and that and his dark eyes full of trepidation.

"What's up?" I asked, rounding the old wet bar I like to use as a counter. "You look all flustered or... you didn't break up with Evie, did you?"

"We broke up weeks ago." He looked up, his eyes brimming with tears. "It's my mom. She's got cancer."

My arms were around him before the first tear dropped and I held him tight as he sobbed. It had been a long time since we had been this close. Mostly I tried to keep my distance, terrified that if we got too close I would want to slip back into the comfortableness of his arms and how easy he had always made life. "When did you find out?" I asked when his sobs subsided a bit.

"Just this morning." He pulled away, dabbing at my shirt with the handkerchief he always carried in his back pocket. Yes, this was my ex, a real 1940s kind of man. "I'm sorry I called you, but I didn't know who else to call."

I pulled his hand away from my shoulder, pulling the hanky out of his hands I dried his cheeks and eyes. "I'm glad you called me," I said, giving the damp rag back to him. "We should go and get something to drink. Maybe have some dinner. Have you eaten? Of course you haven't, you never could eat in a crisis." I had to yell *shut up* in my mind before I could get my mouth to close. "I'm sorry. How is your mom?"

"She's in shock I guess. She didn't say much."

"Well…" The bell over the door chimed. I looked toward the sound and then back to John, giving him my best *I'm sorry* look. "They're here to get a baby carriage. Why don't you go into the office. I'll come get you when I've finished and we'll go across to the pub."

He nodded and made his way back to the tiny closet that housed my antique mahogany desk and a mountain of bills. When the door closed I looked up, that patented smile spread across my now-troubled face.

"How can I… help. You."

He smiled, those pink lips pulling back in that lopsided grin I had always found so endearing. Four years hadn't done anything to ugly him up. "Janey?"

"R-Ryan." Why did I have to stumble? I could feel my smile wavering, but I held my position. "How can I help you?"

"Do you work here?"

"You could say that," I said, happy that he's asked. At least I could correct his assumption that I'd fallen so low I would have to work at a consignment shop. Not that it would be the worst fate. "I own the place."

He nodded. "Very nice."

I looked back at my office, hoping John was okay. "I think so. Now, what can I do for you?"

"Um, I'm supposed to pick up something my sister in law bought today. It's a," he paused, looking over me carefully before finishing with, "carriage."

"Oh, so you're the proud papa almost times two."

He still looked unsure. "Yeah, that's me."

"I heard your little Genevieve is just a *darling*!" I tried not to sound so shrill, but it seemed four years hadn't done much for my sore spot.

"We call her Ginny."

"Of course." I smiled, though I really wanted to punch him square in the jaw. "What's the word?"

He looked stunned. "Word?"

"Your sister in law didn't tell you? She left a word with me that you have to say in order for me to know it's really the right person picking it up." I leaned over the counter, trying to plant the cheekiest smile possible on my face. "What's the word?"

"Oh!" he laughed. Oh, how I had once loved that laugh. "The word would be November, because that is when Kim is due."

"Good job, daddio. The carriage is in the back. Follow me."

It was weird. It had been three years since I had spoken to him, and four years since I had made more than a complete ass of myself at his wedding trying to get him to choose me over her, and now here he was picking up some gift for his wife, about to be a daddy for the second time!

"This might be a little personal," I said as we made our way to the back. "But today your perky little sister in law said that little Ginny just turned three."

"Uh-huh."

"She was pregnant when you married her, wasn't she?"

He stopped and so did I. For a moment we stood in my poorly lit back room in silence. It was different and I don't think it was due to my ex-husband and the looming death of his mother that made it so.

"Yeah."

"Oh." I grabbed the carriage, thrusting it at him. "Is there anything else?" I asked as we made our way to the front door.

"No. I mean, she paid for it, right?"

"With plastic even."

He looked down at me and I felt that old familiar tug. I guess I could have started sliding back into those old familiar feelings. It had been three long years since we had been in the same vicinity, but he had crept back in quite a few times. Here he was, staring down at me with the same blue eyes I had read so many promises in before. I could have misconstrued that long gaze as something romantic. I could have, but my ex-husband had been blessed with a knack for sometimes ruining promising moments.

"Janey," John said from behind the counter.

Ryan looked up, nodding at the man he hadn't ever really liked. "Hey man," he said.

John returned the nod and leaned over the counter, his chin resting on his crooked arm.

"Well, thanks for this," Ryan said, turning his attention back to me. "It was good to see you again."

I nodded. "Yup."

When he was gone and the door was locked I turned on my ex, still standing behind the counter.

"What the hell, John?"

"What, what the hell?"

"Did you have to stand there like a jealous husband?" I made my way around the counter, grabbing my purse and sunglasses. "He's a man picking up a baby carriage for crying out loud!"

"Then why don't you act like it!"

I couldn't believe my ears, nor could I believe my eyes. This was the man who, four years ago, had told me he hadn't loved me for a while, that I was more like a roommate with benefits, acting like a jealous jerk. He *was* a jealous jerk! To say I was livid is only a slight understatement.

"If you didn't need a friend right now I would kick your ass out," I snipped. "Now come on!"

I didn't wait on him. The doorknob had been set to lock automatically when it closed, so there was no need. Instead I stormed out the door and across the street. He followed almost immediately, his head down.

"I'm sorry," he said after a few tense minutes at the dinner table. I had already ordered my first fruity drink and an appetizer, while he had opted for a cold long neck and half my appetizer.

"Sorry, John? For what reason could you *possibly* be sorry? For embarrassing me, perhaps? Or for acting like a friggin caveman?"

"Both." He took a long sip of the golden substance, staring at the bottle when he lowered it as if he were unable to just look at me. "It's just hard as hell to see you still going crazy over that asshole." He took a long, slow sip of his beer. "I guess what's worse is to know that he loves it."

"I wasn't going crazy," I insisted, though I know if he hadn't interrupted I would have been back in that groom room making a fool of myself again.

"Yeah, sure. You never have been able to help yourself with that guy. What kills me is that he doesn't give two shits about you. Never did."

"You don't know that," I mumbled, stifling my pathetic persistence with my cocktail.

"I know this," he said, leaning forward slightly. "If he loved you even an iota of what you've loved him he wouldn't be married. He would be waiting for you. *Pining* for you. You would be in his head non-stop."

"Wow," I said, dipping my head to hide the blush. "Who are you waiting on?"

He looked at me, his dark eyes devouring me like they had in the early days of our marriage.

It didn't take a rocket scientist to decipher that look. "I'm sorry too."

"Why?"

"Just know that I am."

He took another long sip of his beer, his eyes drifting over the people in the pub, but always finding their way back to my face, a face that I should have been hiding in shame. I couldn't stop thinking about all those years. All those years of our marriage that I spent wishing I could be in Ryan's arms, thinking that he loved me even a fraction as hard as I loved him. It was becoming clear, albeit too late, that I, like so many others, had longed for greener pastures, not realizing that I was in the best one.

"Tell me about your mom," I said, taking the first sip of my third fruity drink. "What did the doctor tell her?"

"Sue, you've got cancer." He downed the rest of his second bottle as the waitress dropped off his third.

"Damn." I pushed my hand through the long mop of brown on my own head. "She's only sixty, right?"

"Yeah."

"What is she going to do?"

"She doesn't really know yet. She has another appointment in a couple of days."

"John, I am so sorry." I placed my hand over his and he allowed it, but only for a moment.

Pulling away he grabbed his beer for another long sip. "We'll know more in a week."

I wanted to press on, make him talk about it, but if living with this man for over ten years had taught me anything it was that if he didn't want to talk about something the only thing pressing on could do was cause a massive explosion. His mother, the woman responsible for giving him life was now fighting for hers. No amount of talking, or kind touches would change the loss he was going to experience. I wanted to tell him that not everyone with cancer dies, but that too stayed repressed.

After our fifth and sixth drinks, respectively, we made our way across the street and up to my second floor apartment. It wasn't too bad living above the store, the windows blocked out most of the noise on the weekends and through the week everything was fairly quiet after nine, the floor plan was open with only the one bedroom and bathroom warranting their own private space. It was perfect and I adored the one hundred and fifty year old building to the point of obsession.

John plopped down at the little bistro table I had situated against the window that looked out over my store front, his legs sprawled out in front of him and his head leaned back against the window frame.

I left him there, going into my bedroom to change into a plaid pajama set found at my local goodwill, and to pile my hair into a messy bun. When I made it back into the kitchen he had turned halfway in the chair and was staring out onto the street below.

"Hey," I said, ruffling his hair a bit. It was something I had done in the better years of our marriage. "I'm going to make you a spot on the sofa." I held up the pillow and sheets I had wrestled out of the linen closet to illustrate. "I don't think you should drive home."

He stood up, pulling me into his embrace. "I'm scared," he confessed.

"You should be," I said, returning his hug. "But we'll get you through it. We'll get *her* through it."

He pulled away, brushing a rogue strand of hair away from my face. "You're beautiful," he whispered.

"And you're drunk. Sit down and I'll get the sofa ready." But he didn't listen. Instead he ambled over to the sofa and plopped down.

I slapped the pillow and sheets beside him on the old burgundy sofa and turned to leave.

"I know about the wedding," he said, laying his head against the back.

I stopped cold, unable to even breathe.

"I found the invitation the following Thursday and called the RSVP number. Ryan's sister was all too happy to tell me about what had happened."

I fell into the floral overstuffed chair sitting adjacent to him. "I'm…"

"It didn't take much to put together why you had been acting so strange for that week. I guess that's why I didn't fight it when you said you wanted out. I figured you had never really loved me" He raked a hand through his straw colored hair. "But damn if I didn't still love you."

I started to apologize, to beg him to forgive my ignorance, but a soft rumble began to filter through his open lips.

"I did love you," I whispered, as I pulled the orange and green afghan from the back of the sofa over him. "Just never as much as you deserve."

II.

The store hadn't been open for more than an hour when the door opened and in ambled my somewhat disheveled ex. I made my way into the office, pouring him a tall mug of his favorite coffee. I thought it was the least he deserved after such a terrible day yesterday, so I had dragged my sorry tail out of bed at the ungodly hour of eight and made my way to the market down the way to buy my former husband's favorite brand of coffee.

He grunted slightly when I handed him the mug.

"Sleep well?" I asked, after he had consumed enough to make him human again.

"Not really. I've got a helluva crick in my neck." He raised his hand to massage his problem area.

"I tried to get you to let me make up the sofa, but I guess you're still too good for accepting any help." I made my way around the counter and began to rub the spot his hand had just vacated. "Is that better?"

"Uh-huh," he said, taking a slow sip of his coffee.

When the bell above the door clanged announcing the entrance of my first customer I moved back behind the counter and picked up my latte, something else I had picked up on my stroll back. That was one of the perks of living in the city, easy coffee, but sometimes I just longed for the good ole country silence.

"I thought you didn't like this kind of coffee," he said, leaning up against the counter.

"I don't. I just thought you could use a cup after the day you had yesterday."

He smiled. "Thanks."

I didn't want the moment to end. We hadn't been this civil to one another in quite a while. "So what're you doing today?"

"I've got to get to work." He swallowed the last bit of the ebony liquid.

"After?"

His head fell to the side and his lips pulled back in a smile. "You don't have to do this, Janey," he said.

"Do what?"

"You don't *have* to offer to hang out with me. My mom is sick and it *is* killing me, but I am going to be okay."

Ruby stepped up to the counter, dropping a stack of romance novels on the counter. "Morning," she said.

"Good morning," John offered, though I could tell he was a little irritated that Ruby had interrupted.

The elder women looked at me, giving a sly wink. I laughed, resting my hand on John's shoulder.

"Ruby, this is my *ex*-husband, John. John, this is my *best* customer, Ruby."

"Nice to meet you," he said, extending a hand.

"Nice grip, sonny," Ruby said, her thin lips pulling back in a mischievous grin.

He looked over at me, his eyebrows raising slightly, and pulled his hand away. "Janey, I'll talk to you later," he said, making his way around the counter. "Ruby, you take care."

She didn't speak again until after John had exited the building. There was a part of me wishing she wouldn't open her mouth again because I knew what she would say.

"Do you want to trade these?" I asked, hoping that might sway her.

"*Ex?*" she asked.

"Yes, Ruby," I said. "*Ex.*"

"Why on earth would you throw a hunka burnin love like that out the door?"

I laughed. "A *what?*"

"You heard me. He's a fox."

"And he's a sweetheart too!" Dakota said, waddling up to the counter. She threw her elbow up on the ledge, bending slightly to catch her breath.

Ruby surveyed Dakota, drinking in the image before her. "You don't look so good," she said.

"I'll be fine," Dakota gasped. "The baby is just all up in my diaphragm area."

"Maybe you should sit down," I said, coming around the counter to collect her. "Does Daniel know that you are out gallivanting around instead of resting?"

"I wanted to do a bit of shopping this morning. His birthday is next week and I wanted to get him something special. That, and…"

"And?"

"It's about you-know-who."

Every ounce of self-respect I had saved up over the last four years drained straight out of my body and I found myself pushing Ruby to complete her trade and get out of my store. She was a sweet lady, sometimes, but after our encounter last night my mind was screaming for more knowledge.

That silly 15 year old version of myself was waking up after a long sleep and she needed to be fed. The only thing she craved, of course, was Ryan.

"Okay," I said, plopping down on the chair beside her. "Tuesdays are sporadically busy, so let's do this."

Dakota nodded. "I didn't think I would tell you. I mean, you've worked so hard to get over him. But I know if I don't tell you and you find out you will be pissed at me and never forgive me."

"What is it?" I practically squealed.

"Guess who called me out of the clear blue last night?"

I shrugged.

"Emily."

Her former best friend. She and I had never cared much for one another, but had always managed to keep it civil for Dakota's sake. We both loved her and didn't want to upset her. This is the only reason I bothered to invite her to birthday parties or anything else.

"And what did Emily want."

Of course it was no secret to Dakota that we didn't like one another.

"She called to see how I am and to ask about Danny and the pregnancy. Then she filled me in on what her family is up to. Her kids are growing like weeds and she is working on her second divorce. You know Emily, she doesn't settle for too long. She swears she's single for life now though." Dakota chuckled. Emily was likely to stay single as long as I am likely to not think about Ryan Foust.

"Yeah, right," I snorted.

"Anyway, she told me about her mom and sister. Of course I knew where she was headed. I just waited. Finally she said, and Ryan's wife Kim is having another baby! I tried to act surprised. And I don't think she noticed."

I rolled my eyes.

"She asked how you were doing and I told her about you and John and how you're the proprietress of this fabulous shop. She said she is going to stop by!"

"Did you tell her there is a quaint little shop about five miles from here that might suit her better?"

Dakota laughed. "Anyway, she thought she would end the conversation by saying that she had been thinking of me a lot lately, but never seemed to get around to calling me, and then Ryan called her to tell her he'd seen you, so she decided to give me a call."

This is where my best friend of forever hauled off and gave me a hard smack.

"Ow!" I squealed, nursing my throbbing arm. "What was that for?"

"You didn't bother to tell me that Ryan is Miss Bubbly's brother in law."

"I'm sorry!" I jumped up, thankful when the bell over the door sounded freeing me from her scornful look. Rounding the counter, I met my patron at the display of vintage sunglasses just inside the door. "Welcome to Rags N Bones," I said, attempting to project perkiness. "Can I help you find something?"

The young woman, her belly protruding, looked up with the soft almost-lavender eyes. Immediately I was taken aback by how young she appeared to be versus how far along she seemed to be, and then by the number of pregnant women ambling about in this small town. Of course that latter part of me was being controlled by the green eyed monster that was my jealousy. I'd always wanted a baby. Granted, I'd always wanted that baby with Ryan Foust. And now little miss mouse was on her way to baby number two with him.

"I'm okay," the girl said, her voice as small as her stature.

Brought back from my maddening thoughts, I smiled. "Just let me know if you need anything."

I managed to maintain my smile while I crossed back over to Dakota. I knew without a doubt she had been surveying me from the distance, and I also knew that she had been keenly aware of the moment my inner demon had awakened.

Was I a goner again?

"You okay?" Dakota asked.

"Sure. Why wouldn't I be?"

Her lips pulled back into a half smile/ half frown. "Do you want to cry?"

I shook my head, but no matter how much force I put into that shake my eyes wouldn't stop blurring.

Dakota stood up, gathering me the best she could into her embrace. "It's okay, honey," she soothed. "I'm sorry."

"I'm fine," I said, pulling away. "I'm fine. There are more pressing matters in this world than Ryan Foust." Grabbing a kleenex from the box on the counter I dabbed at my eyes. "I am just so furious with myself." I plopped down, dropping my hands in my lap. "I thought I'd come so far only to find that one chance encounter sends me crashing again."

"You're not crashing," Dakota said. "You're just dealing. It takes time." She leaned over, kissing the top of my head. "I love you, doofus."

I laughed. "I love you too, be-snotch."

Dakota feigned hurt, placing her hands on either side of her abdomen as if to block her unborn child from such language. She laughed. "I have to get. I've got a doctor thing. Call me later?"

I nodded.

"Hey," she said, her plump hand reaching out to me. "You need to face it before you can get past it."

"What does that mean?" I whined. Even I was becoming annoyed with myself.

"You can't crash his wedding, be devastated, and then think because you immerse yourself in *things* that you're over it. You have to figure out why it is so easy for him to pull you back in. And without even trying at that!"

"Oh, he was trying. If John hadn't interrupted us who knows what would have happened." I knew it was a silly teenage dream even as the words came spilling out, but I couldn't stop them. This was the process. This was *my* process.

"Really?" Dakota said.

I shook my head. "Maybe. I don't know. I always see things that aren't there." I waved her on. "Go ahead, get out of here. I'm terribly busy and you have your doctor appointment. Let me know what the doc says, okay?"

She nodded, but I could tell she didn't want to leave. She felt bad for feeling compelled to mention him, though she was right in assuming I would have been pissed had I found out she didn't tell me. He called his cousin, one of the very few links between him and me. I couldn't help reading into that. Who wouldn't?

When I was alone in my shop again I found myself pulling over to the little desk in the back office, searching through my social networking site for the one friend that was a mutual friend of both me and Ryan. He's less than social, but his wife is on the opposite side of that spectrum. When I didn't find him I put in Kim's name and there she was.

Sometimes I wondered if she put happy daddy pictures as her profile pics just to show me that he is happy with her and there would never be a place for me in his heart. Of course, I always squelch that with the fact that I had his heart first. At least I think I did.

And there he was, his little darling hoisted up on his broad shoulders, with a big doofy grin on his face and happiness in his eyes. I guess I should have been okay with seeing that happiness, but, truth is, it hurt like hell every time I saw him happy with anyone other than me.

Yes, I knew at that moment how big a basket case I really am. Actually, before that moment, but I am learning not to dally.

"What're you doing?" John asked from in front of the counter.

I jumped, hating the haste I used to minimize my current screen. "John," I squealed. "You scared the life out of me!"

He surveyed me carefully

"What?"

"Why do you look like you're guilty of something?" he asked, rounding the corner.

"I don't." Reaching down I pressed the button to shut down the computer (incorrectly, I know) and stood up. "So what're you doing here?"

"You told me to come by later so we could hang." He shook his head. "You were just being nice. I should have realized. Sorry, we've just been apart so long I don't know you as well as I used to."

"I *did* mean it!" I said, trying to steer him clear of the wreckage that was this particular conversation. "I just thought you were coming after closing. I will still be here for a couple of hours. Do you want to hang out in the loft for a bit?"

"No. I'll go home and change. Maybe I will treat you to something nice."

I smiled. "Sounds like a date or somethin." He used to like my silly girl persona, and judging by the smile on his face he still did.

"Or somethin," he said. "I'll see you around seven. Be ready."

"Always," I said, completely conscious of the blush creeping into my cheeks.

A blush! My ex-husband just made me blush. I had forgotten he could do that.

III.

I had decided that a date with my ex warranted the early 1990s throwback I had been saving for a special occasion. A long flowing flower tunic, made of the sheerest material, coupled with a long black skirt, black suit vest (unbuttoned) and doc martins. My flapper cap with a hug paisley flower completed the look. Surveying myself in the mirror, I turned from side to side. Maybe the vest was too much.

The sound of the doorbell ended my inner turmoil, and I bounced through the living area, pulling open the door with dramatic flair.

He didn't say anything at all as his eyes traveled from my head to my toes and back up again. He'd always loved long skirts, a fact that I most certainly kept in mind when choosing my ensemble.

"Nice outfit."

I laughed. "I knew you wouldn't appreciate it as much as I do." He held out a bouquet of wildflowers and I took them, crushing them to my nose so that I might stifle a whimper.

I'd also forgotten how romantic he could be.

"They're beautiful," I said. "Let me put them in some water and we can go."

John had never been the kind of man that liked to be kept waiting. He was a *let's get this over with* kind of guy, so instead of selecting the perfect vase I filled a glass with water and plopped the purples, oranges, and reds in, telling my inner self that there would be time to select a vase later.

Though I did know of the perfect one down in the shop. What better way to showcase its beauty than with that of the bouquet?

"Wow," he said, sliding the book he'd been flipping through back in the shelf when I stopped by the front door. "I expected that to take longer."

"I know you don't like to wait, so I decided to put them in a mason jar for now."

"All I do is wait," he mumbled as he walked past me and out the door.

I contemplated asking what he meant, but my mouth didn't open. I guess I was afraid of what his answer might be. Instead, I locked the door and led the way downstairs to the street.

His beat up pickup truck was waiting for us by the curb, but he surprised me when he slid his arm around my waist and led me down the street.

I knew we would end up at Tres Chic, a silly little bistro a couple of blocks from my shop. It wasn't very chic at all, but the food was good and the atmosphere even better. It wasn't until I heard the bass about a block away that I realized this was their live jazz night. Samantha, the hippie chick that owned the bistro, was all about live music, and even more about live jazz.

Yes, he still knew my weaknesses.

"John!" I gave him a huge hug. "I haven't listened to live jazz in *such* a long time!"

He shrugged. "I saw a flyer on my way home and thought it would be perfect."

I gave him a quick pop kiss on the cheek. "You were right," I whispered.

We were seated quickly (a perk of knowing the owner) in a table just left of the stage in the corner. It was quiet enough for us to be able to speak, but still close enough to become lost in the sound.

We ordered a bottle of sweet table wine (my favorite) and appetizers. At Tres Chic you had your choice of breadsticks or fried pickles for appetizers. We chose the former as opposed to the latter. Pickles and sweet wine do not mesh.

I took a sip of the wine, letting the taste of muscadine spread over my tongue and slowly down my throat, and then I smiled. I don't know why, but this felt like one of the earlier times in our marriage. Maybe it was the familiarity of it all. Which, I realize, is precisely why I have tried to remain distant from my ex. "Why haven't we done this before?" I asked.

He took a sip of the wine, his mouth twisting a bit. He was definitely not a wine man.

"And why didn't you order a beer?" I laughed.

"To the first question, I think you know," he said, attempting another taste. "To the second, I have no idea." He laughed and held up his glass to the waiter, ordering a bottleneck when the young man ambled over.

"Right away, sir," the twenty-something said, rushing off.

I couldn't help picturing a tiny rodent scampering away, though I'm sure he wouldn't appreciate the comparison.

Anxious to steer clear of the uncomfortable conversation of who was at fault for what, since I'd been so brilliant as to bring up why we hadn't hung out with one another for a while, I decided to move the focus. "So, why did you and Evie break up?"

He took the chilled bottle being delivered by the boy wonder with a smile, nodding his thanks. After taking a swig of the golden liquid inside he shrugged. "She wanted something I couldn't give."

When he looked as though he was not going to provide anything further I asked, "Which is?"

He shrugged again. "I don't know. I thought I was giving her everything she wanted and needed, but I tend to think I am giving more than I am. I guess."

"That's not fair," I said. "To me or her. She was a good kid. Stupidly optimistic, but good."

He laughed. "She does love a silver lining."

I refilled my glass. "So is this my fault too?"

"I didn't say that," he said a little too sharp. Then, as if he'd caught his own tone he said softer, "I didn't say that at all."

We were quiet through the main course. The jazz and wine had lulled me into a sort of quasi-romantic kind of mood. He must have sensed it because after we'd finished he stood up, pulling me out onto the dance floor to take a turn to *This Love of Mine*. Too bad Ella wasn't there to supply the lyrics.

"How's your mom? Did you talk to her today?" I asked, longing for some conversation to break up the romance. In no time I knew I would be putty in his hands. If I know my ex (and I do), I suspected that was exactly his plan. I needed to get back to reality. What was my purpose with him? Friends. His mom has cancer and he needs a friend. A shoulder to cry on. Or lean on. Or whatever.

"She's a little better today," he said. I could tell that he wanted to steer clear of the reality speak.

"No word from the doctor?"

"I told you it would be a week. It's only been two days."

"I was being optimistic," I said with a wink.

He laughed. "Why don't you leave the optimism to Evie?"

He wanted to kiss me as much as I wanted to kiss him. I could see it in those deep onyx orbs. But he didn't. Instead he whirled me back to our table and I, without an ounce of grace, plopped down.

"It's getting late," he said, after I downed the rest of my glass. "You ready?"

I nodded.

On the walk back to my apartment I didn't say anything at all. Instead I formulated exactly what my next steps would be. If I gave in to my current thought process I would jump his bones at my doorstep. If I remained rational, a talent that was quickly fading at this point (or had it hightailed it out hours ago) I would tell him goodnight at the door and that would be the end of it.

The old Chevy came into sight and my knees became like jello. I knew what move I would make, and I knew that would change the whole of the game. However, just when I was about to open my mouth and expel my proposition, John stopped.

Jostled by the suddenness of it all, I stumbled. "What..." I stopped when my eyes fell on the front doors to my shop. "Ryan?"

His lips pulled back in a lop-sided grin and I could feel John's posture change. Suddenly the romance of the evening slid away and I realized my ex-husband was standing mere feet away from the man that had, effectively, ruined his marriage.

"R-Ryan," I said, breaking away from John. I figured if I put myself between them John would be less likely to make a fool out of both of us. "What are you doing here? It's almost midnight."

"Hey, John," he said, acknowledging the man fuming behind me. I knew from the twinkle in his eye he was amused by the apparent discomfort he continued to cause John.

"Hey," John managed.

Ryan smiled. "I had to work late tonight, but I needed to come by the store. I forgot something very important in there and I can't go home until I retrieve it."

"What is it?"

He pushed away from the building and I was transported back to the day I'd met him fifteen years before.

"I-it couldn't wait until tomorrow?"

"It's *very* important."

I looked at John, really hating that he would never really be rid of Ryan. Yes, I know how self-important that makes me seem. I can't help it though, that is exactly what I thought. "John, do you mind going up…"

He shook his head. "I'll see you later, Janey. Just let me know when you've come back down to planet Earth."

And there it was. The jab that I had felt coming from the nano second we'd noticed Ryan standing against my building. As if John had anything to worry about. As if he should worry at all. After all, we hadn't been husband and wife for quite some time.

Ryan nodded to him, that cocky grin never leaving his face.

"Why did you do that?" I asked as I pulled out my keys to open the old door.

"Why did I do what?" Ryan asked, standing far too close for my own comfort.

How was I supposed to concentrate with the unattainable so close?

"Gloat. You always used to do that. I would have thought you'd grown beyond it by now."

Ryan laughed. "I have no idea what you're talking about."

"I'm sure." I closed the door, sliding the lock in place. He looked back, first at the door and then to me, raising his eyebrow a bit. "Don't worry," I said. "I don't plan to defile you. I just don't want anyone waltzing in and walking off with my inventory."

He didn't believe me, but I couldn't blame him. I didn't even believe me.

"So what did you leave here?" I asked. I was having the most surreal moment of my life. Here I was alone with the guy I spent countless hours longing for and I couldn't figure out whether I wanted to jump his bones or kick him.

Dakota would have told me to do the latter, I'm sure.

"One of the front wheels to that carriage I picked up. I got to my sister in law's house and couldn't find it."

"Okay." I definitely wanted to kick him. "Let's go check the store room. That seems like the most likely place."

"So, I thought you two were divorced," Ryan said, as we began to look through the boxes lining the floor in the store room.

"We are," I said, digging through my most recent purchase. It had been at an estate sale a couple of counties over.

Lots of costume jewelry and vintage clothing. Nothing that would fit me though. Damn skinny women.

"Then why has he been here every time I have come in?"

"First, you've only been in twice. Second, he's going through a hard time. I'm being there for him."

Deciding that the wheel was not in the current box, I pushed that one to the side and grabbed another.

"It looked like you two were about to *rekindle* something out there."

I dropped the clothing I was currently sifting through and looked at him. "What does that have to do with your baby's carriage?"

"It was just an observation."

I stared at him, loving the way the dim light bounced off the red and gold of his hair. It was longer than normal. Long enough to really pull. I couldn't help the vision that presented itself in my mind. One of Ryan and myself all wrapped up in one another, my hands full of that hair. Shaking my head, I shoved my box to the side and grabbed another.

"What were you thinking just then?" he asked.

"Nothing," I answered, unable to look at him. Something told me he would figure it out and if he did I would never recover from the humiliation. "Maybe it went under the shelf."

I jumped up to my knees and began trying to peer underneath the steel structure. "I have lost tons of things under here. I never thought I would get them back."

"Janey," he whispered.

I stopped looking, but was too terrified to turn around to him. There were warning bells and whistles going off in my head. *Get out, girl! Run!* But instead of listening, I fell back on my haunches and looked at him.

"I didn't lose the wheel," he confessed. "It's on the carriage at my sister in law's house."

I couldn't speak. Part of me was terrified that I would become that sad little person I had embodied for so long. Always waiting for him to acknowledge me. Always waiting for him to beg me to be with him. I'd had countless fantasies of what might happen if the two of us ended up alone in a room together with no one to know what transpired beyond us and the walls.

"Then why are you here, Ryan?" I said at last. "And why do you have me digging through boxes and under dusty shelves to find something you haven't lost?"

"I just wanted to see you again," he said.

I stood up, dusting away the massive amount of dirt I had managed to gather. "What?"

He stood as well, hovering over me by several inches. He was too close again. I tried to step back, but he caught my arm, holding me in place.

"I don't think this is the best thing for us to be doing, Ryan," I breathed. It was too close. We were too close.

I was slipping away and could do nothing to stop myself.

He raised a hand to my cheek and I wanted to pull away, but I was held there. Part of me wondering if I had passed out. Would I wake up in my bed stunned by the intimacy of my dream? It wouldn't have been the first time.

"I felt like shit when you came into my room at the chapel. When you called me out and poured your heart out I felt… devastated."

"Not devastated enough to not get married," I said, finally finding the strength to pull away.

"I told you, she was pregnant," he said, his voice strained.

"And she's pregnant now. So what's the difference? Does one make you want to get married and the second one make you want to cheat on your wife?"

"It's not mine," he whispered.

I knew it was a lie. I hated him for lying to me, but I hated myself more for trying to believe him. If she was carrying another man's baby then it would be okay for them to do whatever they did tonight. This moment would be theirs. I couldn't help but romanticize it all.

I think he knew that.

"You have to go," I said.

He looked stunned. "What? Janey, I don't want to go home."

I found myself becoming hopelessly angry over the entire situation. I mean, why was the universe having such sport with me lately? First, my ex-husband shows up after months of no contact utterly devastated by the possibility that his mother might be taken from him. Then Ryan shows up. My Kryptonite. John starts to woo me and now Ryan… Well, I honestly had no idea what he was trying to do.

Did he think that I would jeopardize a marriage? Did he think that I would allow myself to be the cause of unhappiness for his little girl and the new child that was soon to enter this world?

I might have been that girl on the day of his wedding, so pathetic and desperate to have him that I would throw everything asunder, but that was not me at this point.

He stroked my cheek, brushing stray strands away from my face. "I feel so different when I'm around you. You make me want to be that boy I was fifteen years ago."

"Well I don't want to be that girl," I said pulling away. "I played that part far too long."

"I think about you…"

"Really, Ryan?" How could he be so insensitive? "So what am I supposed to do now? Am I supposed to be the gullible sap that allows you to lead me on? Are we supposed to do this tonight, whatever *this* is, and have me watch you walk out the door and back to your wife?"

"I…"

"How often do you *really* think about me, Ryan?" I questioned, now in full rant. Part of me, a much smaller part now, was screaming for my mouth to close and just allow this to happen. How long did I wish for this? How long did I fantasize that he would come back to me and want to be with me? Too long.

"I thought you wanted me too."

No answer to the question. My irrational self screamed at the insignificant little girl sobbing in my head. It was as though I had developed some sort of split personality, both able to interact with one another. It's time to grow up, I told her. It's time to move on from what would have never amounted to anything.

"I thought I did," I answered, strangely calm. "I have been a fool for you. I wanted so badly for you to want me that I discarded the only man who truly loved me. I went to your wedding and made a *complete* fool of myself. It didn't matter to you then. And I suspect that it doesn't really matter to you now."

"You're wrong."

He grabbed me then, crushing his full lips to mine. He was my kryptonite.

IV.

It was 5:30 in the morning when my phone rang. Dakota was on the other end screaming in pain. The baby was ready and she was alone. I didn't ask where Daniel was. Sadly, it didn't even occur to me. Instead I instructed her to call an ambulance, knowing they would make it to her before I would.

Stumbling in the twilight I jerked on the nearest t-shirt and jeans I could find and made my way out into the morning. Life has such a way about it.

My phone rang as I was en route and I was not surprised to find John's name staring up at me. "Hey," I answered. "What's up?"

"You're up early," he said. "I was just going to leave a message for you."

"An angry message?"

He laughed. "No. I'm a big boy, Janey, and we're not married anymore. You can do whatever you want with whomever you want."

"Yeah. Well, I didn't." I don't know why I told him. It wasn't any of his business.

But I did know exactly why I'd told him.

"Oh. W-well, if you did it's fine."

I laughed. "Shut up. You know I'm not going to lie to you."

After a few moments of silence he asked, "So what're you doing today?"

"I'm going to the hospital right now. Dakota is in labor."

"Really?"

"Yes." I smiled at his silence. He'd known Dakota longer than I had. His big brother affection had always been endearing. "I could use some coffee," I offered, giving him the excuse he needed to check on her.

"What about Danny? Who's taking care of him?"

"He's with Dakota's sister. It's all under control. Now, are you bringing me coffee, or not?"

"Yes. Bye."

I laughed as I put the phone away and pulled into the lot of the hospital.

"Hey," Dakota said when I walked into her birthing room.

"Hey," I said, giving her a quick peck on the head. "How's it going?"

She shrugged. "Eh."

We both laughed. She was nervous, which made me nervous. With Danny she'd been very gung ho, let's have this kid, but with this one she'd been quiet. And I couldn't help but notice, more cautious.

"What's the doctor saying?"

"Not much. She just came in and violated me, then stepped out."

I smoothed back her hair. "You're scared. Is everything okay?"

"Yeah. Everything's fine."

"Dakota,"

She looked at me, her blue eyes filled to the brim. "I've been under some stress with this one."

"What? Why?"

"Daniel left me," she sobbed.

"What? You can't be serious. When? Why didn't you tell me?"

"I'm sorry. I just couldn't."

I smoothed her hair back, kissing her forehead. Stunned didn't even begin to cover it. How could she not tell me? How could I not ask how things with Daniel were going? I tried to remember the last time I asked about him, but there was no recollection. "Have you called him? To let him know, I mean."

She shook her head.

"Ma'am," a nurse said. "You'll have to leave now. We're taking her in to surgery."

"Surgery?" I looked at Dakota. She was devastated. "I am so sorry," I said. "Everything will be fine." I kissed her head. "I'll call Daniel. Everything will be fine."

Dakota nodded.

"I'll be here when you get out," I promised, backing out of the room.

It is hard to describe the thoughts racing through my mind as I stared down at Daniel's name on the face of my phone. Should I call him? My mind couldn't help but race to a million conclusions that could or could not be true.

Was he cheating on Dakota?

Was he just overwhelmed with the prospect of doing the daddy thing again?

Did he just decide that he's not husband/daddy material?

I was angry and sad and all mixed up again. Only this time it was for a perfectly good reason. I should have seen how stressed she was, yet I'd allowed myself to become all wrapped up in Ryan Foust. Again.

"Hello?"

"Daniel, it's Janey."

"Oh. Hey. What's up?"

I wanted to slam him with questions. Why did you leave my best friend? Why did you abandon your son? Why have you abandoned your unborn child? But instead I said, "Dakota is being taken back to surgery."

"What? When? What's wrong?" His concern was endearing.

"I don't know why. All I know is they made me leave the room and said they were taking her back."

"I'll be right there."

The phone went dead and I sagged against the wall.

"What's up?" John asked from behind me.

I turned toward him, unable to stop the tears that had been blurring my vision from spilling forth. He looked so helpless, standing there with a cup of coffee in each hand. I don't know how he managed it, but in seconds I was in his embrace.

"What's wrong? Is Dakota okay?"

I turned my head up to look at him. "I don't know if she's okay," I said. "Because I am a terrible friend."

"No, you're not," He soothed. "Come on." He led me over to the small sofa into the private waiting room just off the main hall. I imagined that this was the room they escorted the families to when there were complications. The irony being that all of life is complicated. "Tell me what's going on," he said, his tone tender. This was his caregiver tone.

"Everything is a mess. Evidently Dakota has had a tough pregnancy, Daniel left her, and I am an ass."

He laughed in spite of himself. "Please tell me you're not just figuring that last bit out."

I shoved him, but was thankful he was trying to alleviate my worries. "If I hadn't been so wrapped up in other things I would have asked her how she was doing and wouldn't have accepted her weak excuse the other day when she was in my shop. Instead I was too wrapped up in…"

"Ryan," he finished.

"And you." I was ashamed that Ryan was the first thought that had come into his mind.

"You don't have to say that, Janey. It's okay."

I shook my head. "It's true, John. Truth is, I thought I was so damned confused again. I was starting to turn on my head, but then last night I had this moment of clarity. I was on my knees in the dim light of my store room with Ryan and I…"

He stood up. "Janey, I can be a supportive friend to a point, but I can't listen to you talk about him."

"But,"

"I'm sorry. I know this isn't the time for this, but if I hear his name again.."

"You brought him up!"

"No, that's not true."

"Yes, it is, John. I didn't mention him."

"You don't have to *mention* him, Janey. He's always in the damn room! For eleven years he was always there. That's why when you left me I decided not to fight for you to come back. A man can only live so long in another man's shadow. But I thought after all this time you might have moved on." He dragged a hand through the mop on his head. "I thought you might finally have room for *me* in there." He pointed to my heart, then shook his head. I wanted him to go forward. Maybe if we got past this unpleasantness we might actually be able to get on with our lives. He'd never properly told me off for being unfaithful to him with my heart and my mind. Now was as good a time as any. "I am not going to do this right now," he said after an excruciatingly long silence. "Dakota needs you. This day is not about us. It's about her. Try to keep that in mind."

"What?" I stood up. "Are you insinuating that I am incapable of concentrating on my friend? On today of all days."

"I have to go."

I didn't call him back. I knew he wouldn't come back. I told you, he's a 1940s kind of guy. If he says he's not going to talk about something he's not going to do it.

If Daniel hadn't shown up I'm quite certain I would have fallen into a pit of despair, but not knowing exactly why he had left my friend I wouldn't be a puddle of sadness around him. Instead, I put all of my energy into Dakota. Something that I realize I should have done from the beginning.

"Hey," Daniel said, taking a seat in the waiting room. "Why are you in here? Is there something wrong?"

"No," I answered. "I mean, I don't know. I haven't heard anything."

"When did she go back?"

"When I called you."

He moved to the windows, his gaze falling out over the old town he'd only moved to for Dakota. We didn't speak again.

Hours later the nurse finally came into the waiting room to let us know that Dakota and baby were doing fine. Cordially, Daniel and I chatted as we made our way into the room they'd assigned her to. There was talk of the weather and John's mother. He asked how the shop was doing and how my own mother was doing. I answered him simply, afraid that if I allowed myself too many words I would ask one of the questions burning in my mind.

Dakota's bed was raised and in her arms rested her precious bundle. "Hey," she whispered when she saw us.

"Hey," Daniel said, going immediately to his wife's side. "I'm so sorry I wasn't here," he whispered. "I wanted to be there with you when she was born."

"I know," Dakota said, her voice shaking. "We got through it though. I imagine there will be more difficult times."

He looked back at me and I knew that he was too uncomfortable to speak while I was present.

"I'll be out of your way as soon as I see my girls," I said. Moving to the opposite side of Dakota's bed, I kissed her head and looked down at the bundle in her arms. "She's beautiful," I said.

"Thank you," Dakota whispered. I knew she was thanking me for calling Daniel.

"No problem, chick." I looked at Daniel, smiling slightly. "You both did good. Again."

They laughed in unison. It was something they always did. I wouldn't have suspected anything was amiss by seeing them together with their precious daughter. He was an over-the-moon dad and she was a glowing mom. How could something that looks so perfect be broken?

"I'd better get going," I said.

"Really?" Dakota said, though I could see that she was looking forward to some alone time.

"Yeah. I'd better give the new parents some time alone with her before everyone else starts showing up."

V.

It was almost five when I pulled up in front of the house I used to occupy with my husband. It was strange to see it now after all this time. The last time I'd even set eyes on it was about a year after the divorce. Some sense of nostalgia had settled over me and I'd driven out here to do nothing more than stare at a ghost. My house was a ghost.

John had been with someone at that point. It was more of something to occupy his time. What else would he have done with a twenty year old girl? One summer of hot sex and then she was off to college again and he slid back into the life of an almost middle aged man.

After the third buzz the door flew open. He looked like hell. He also looked none-too-pleased to see me. "You'd better have a damn good reason for laying on that bell," he snapped.

"I think we need to talk," I said. "Now."

He moved to the side, allowing me to step into the open foyer. It had been one of my favorite things about the house when we'd bought it. Closing the door, he led me straight back to the kitchen.

"Smells good," I said as the aroma of stewed beef and potatoes filled my senses.

"You're welcome to have some," he said removing the lid of the slow cooker to stir the concoction. "You know I always make too much." Opening the cupboard he took out two bowls. Removing the lid of the cooker once more he scooped a helping into each one and placed them on the counter, one for him and one for me.

"Thank you."

"Drink?"

"Beer is fine."

He grabbed two long necks out of the ice box and held one out for me, then grabbed his bowl and made his way over to the breakfast nook and the first table we'd purchased as a couple. I followed.

"Needs more pepper," he mumbled.

He knew what I expected and this was his way to work up to it. It was one of the qualities that had worn me down over the years. Why couldn't he just come out with it? Why did he have to work up to it? Of course I know why. He's not good with emotional stuff. That's probably why he was still here and not with his mother.

"I think it's delicious," I said, knowing he would hate that.

He put his spoon down. "Why are you here, Janey? I thought you would be with Dakota."

"Daniel's with her."

"I thought he left her?"

"He did. I think." I shrugged. "Truth is, I have no idea. They seemed so normal. I wouldn't have known anything was wrong if she hadn't told me."

"You didn't ask him?"

"No." I took a swig from my bottle. "I decided to take some advice. Even if it was given quite rudely."

He shook his head.

"What?" I asked.

"You're going to make me do this, aren't you?"

"Do what?"

He looked up at me. "What happened last night?"

"We went out on a great date and you almost got lucky."

"You know what I mean," he said, taking a swig of his own. "What happened with your one true love?"

It was a stab and it hurt like one, but he had every right. He'd put up with a lot over the years. Especially where Ryan Foust was concerned.

"I don't know to whom you are referring."

"What happened with Ryan after I left?" he snipped. Then he stood up, shaking his head. "Never mind, I don't want to know."

"I want you to know," I said, moving over to him.

"Why?" He looked at me and my heart broke a little. "Why was he even there? I thought he was married and his wife is expecting."

"You are correct on both counts," I said. "He told me that he'd lost the wheel to the baby carriage his sister in law bought from me. But I don't think we should move that far with the conversation just yet."

"What?"

"You were saying something to me at the hospital and I think I owe it to you to let you finish."

"I said everything I needed to. I shouldn't have said that much."

I moved in front of him, placing one hand on each side of his face. "What you said was true, John, and I am so sorry that I caused you such pain and made you feel like you could never matter. I was foolish in so many ways."

He tried to pull away.

"I am not asking you to take me back. I don't deserve a man like you, but I believe that I owe you this. Last night Ryan came to my shop with the intentions of cheating on his wife. I have been so pathetic where he is concerned that he thought I would be putty in his hands. We were in my storeroom on our knees searching for something he'd never lost. That's when it hit me. All those years I'd been doing the same thing, searching for something in him that I'd never lost. Still living in the silly dreams of a teenage girl! When he kissed me all I could think about were the years I'd wasted on him when I could have put all that energy into you. I'd cheated myself. Most of all, though, I cheated you. You didn't deserve to be treated as second-best." I took a deep breath. "I can't take back the years you lost waiting on me. But I can say that I am truly sorry for not loving you the way you deserve to be loved."

I wanted to kiss him. I think I may have actually leaned in to do so, but the previous night and that look on Ryan's face as he did the same thing to me stopped me. I didn't want to be the pompous ass thinking I could have my way with someone simply because they had feelings for me.

"Thank you for dinner," I whispered. "Keep me updated on your mom. And if you need anything let me know." I hugged him. "See you around."

I probably shouldn't have run out of there so fast. I'm sure to the neighbors I looked like a mad woman. Not that they hadn't been used to seeing me disheveled at one time. I managed to hold back my heaving sobs until I was at the mouth of my old street. Waiting on the passing traffic I began to heave and sob. I'd lost everything in the past twenty-four hours. The man I should have never loved and the one I should have. Not to mention the loss of that little girl I'd held so tightly to.

"Time to grow up," I said as I pulled into traffic and made my way home. "You're definitely a big girl now."

VI.

Dakota leaned over, offering the binky to her precious Amelie. We'd just celebrated her two week mark with biscotti and mochas, while Miss Amelie had celebrated with breast milk and a burp cloth.

"How are things going?" I asked. "Between you and Daniel, I mean."

Dakota smiled. "I don't know. He comes over every night to see the kids, but we don't talk much. He tells me that he loves me, but he just can't be with me right now. I just don't understand what is wrong with him."

"But it's not another woman?"

"He says it's not, but he's said a lot of things."

I covered her hand with my own. "I'd like to take Danny this weekend, if you don't mind. I'm going out to my sister's and her kids love him."

"Why don't we both go?" she offered. "I love your sister. And her kids."

I laughed. "You don't love her kids. You think they're spoiled and annoying."

"They are spoiled and annoying," Dakota said. "But we need to get out of the house. All of us."

"Okay, but if you change your mind let me know. I'll even take little Amelie." I looked at her. "I'm sorry I wasn't there for you."

"We've talked about this, Janey," she said with a smile. "You're always there for me. Now, tell me what happened with

Ryan. I've been so busy for the last two weeks I haven't even thought to harass you about the night he showed up at your shop."

I groaned. "Absolutely nothing happened. Not that he didn't want it to."

"He is such slime."

"I know." I took a sip of my steaming café. "He lied to get me alone. I would have hooked up with John that night if Ryan hadn't been standing at my door."

"What!"

"Yes, ma'am. John and I went out on a date that night. We were both a little buzzed and I was just about to make my move on him when Ryan reared his pretty head."

"John was pissed," she said with glee.

"To say the least. But he left and I brought Ryan inside to find the wheel to the baby carriage his twig of a sister in law bought for his little wifey."

"Careful," Dakota warned.

"I guess it's habit," I said with a laugh. "Or maybe I am just allowing the younger me to have her bitter feelings."

"Let's hope that's all. Continue."

"Well, we went back into the storeroom and I was trying to find the wheel so that I could get him away from me. I was irritated that he'd shown up so late and ruined my evening with John. And then he started coming onto me."

"Oh my gosh."

"But you would be proud, D. Well, not at first. I could feel myself buying into it all. His touches and the tone of his voice. I could feel that sad little girl trying to take control of me. But then I got mad. I'm not even sure what it was that made me so mad."

"How did his majesty take that?"

I laughed. "I'm afraid he was quite shocked." I took another sip and then said, "I was too. I started yelling at him. And then he kissed me."

"*What?*"

"Yeah. And it was good." I closed my eyes. My mind transporting me back to that night two weeks before when I was standing in my shop with Ryan Foust's tongue darting in and out of my mouth.

My arms slid around his neck and I leaned into him, allowing the heat of that kiss to slide over me like a warm wave. My body was more than receptive to the idea of him having his way with me. And why wouldn't it be? I had consumed quite a few drinks at dinner. But then my mind snapped. I guess that's how you might describe it. I went from being upset to warm to totally pissed.

I jerked away from him. He was shocked, to say the very least. He even stumbled for a second.

"Janey, what are you…"

"I'm not that girl anymore, Ryan" I said. "If you thought you could get me alone and use my most humiliating moment in order to get me naked you have been mistaken. When I walked into that room I was a completely different person than I am today. I was pathetic. I was living in a fantasy of my own creation. Truth is, I don't like you. How could I possibly like a man who leads me on for years only to leave me to languish in the despair of my own making? If you'd been honest with me even once I could have been spared the humiliation of loving you. Get out of my shop. And don't ever come here again."

"It sounds like your blood was probably boiling," Dakota said, bringing me back to the present.

"I had to lie down," I said with a chuckle. "Two days later he sent me flowers."

"He did not!"

"He did."

"No card though, right?"

"There was a card. It just said '*Sorry*' and his initials."

Dakota shook her head. "Coward."

"You've got that right."

"What about John?"

I shrugged.

Amelie, from her little basket to her mother's right, began to cry out and I felt glad that she'd saved me from explaining how I'd managed to muck that one up.

"I'd better get her home," Dakota said gathering her things. "I'm running out of milk and will need to pump soon."

"Alright, mama," I said, helping her get everything out to the car.

Once Amelie was fastened into place Dakota wrapped her arms around me. "I love you, Janey."

"I'm glad someone does."

Dakota smiled, her eyes settling on something behind me. "I don't think I'm the only one," she said.

I turned to find John standing by the front door of my shop, hands shoved in his pockets. He was slouching and his hair looked as if he hadn't brushed it in a week. "He's nervous," I whispered to my friend.

"Go get him, girl," Dakota said giving me a shove. "Hi, John! Bye, John!" she said, making her way around to her door.

He smiled, giving her a wave.

"Where have you been?" I asked after Dakota's old Impala had pulled away.

"I went to visit my mom."

"What did the doctor say?"

"He's optimistic that they caught it early enough."

"That's good news," I said, happy to see the relief on his face.

"Yeah. We were happy to have a bit of hope." He nodded toward the direction Dakota had gone. "How about her?"

"Dakota? She's fine. She's making it. I have hope for them." I shifted. "Do you want to go inside?"

"No," he answered, his expression taking on a serious but extremely hesitant expression. This was his make it or break it face.

"So, to what do I owe this pleasure?" I asked, unable to help the anticipation that began to bubble within. I have always been a little too hopeless in the romance department.

"Did you mean all that?" he asked.

"Every word."

"Because if you didn't…"

"Every last word," I reiterated.

His eyes fell over me and I couldn't stop myself from smoothing my hair and adjusting my late 90s frock. "You look great," he said.

I smiled. "Thank you."

"And Ryan?" he asked. "Because I can't go through that again."

"What are you saying, John?"

A dozen butterflies had been unleashed and I could feel my insides fluttering. Nerve endings fired up in anticipation of what I hoped he would say. Was he here to consent to a second chance for us? For me? Did I deserve a second chance?

Of course I knew that I didn't, but it didn't stop me from saying a silent prayer that I would be granted one.

He placed one hand on each side of my face and leaned down, his lips covering mine.

He is my kryptonite.

Moving On

You sit in the brown and white overstuffed chair common in most little jive coffee places, settling in with intentions to concentrate on the book you've been trying to read for a week; only three more chapters to go and not a lot of time before this solace would be interrupted with more frantic Saturday morning chores. Placing your oversized bag on the floor by your right foot, you lean back, delicately balancing the iced latté with yummy whipped cream and a drizzle of chocolate syrup, and the trials of Anita Shreve's newest heroine in one hand, as you attempt to straighten your favorite denim skirt with the other. You are mid-straightening when your eyes drift across the coffee colored tiles to the table by the windows. For a moment you contemplate bolting, just grabbing your bag (book and latte be damned) and running as fast as you can away from this scenario that reeked with disaster, but you were frozen in place, unable to do anything beyond stare.

There, dressed in tattered jeans and a faded band shirt, is the first guy you ever gave your heart to. He's sipping a cup of what you assume is coffee (he's really a no frills kind of guy) and his right ankle is resting on his left knee. He looks so contented sitting there sipping his grande whatever, and yucking it up with his wife.

You know she's his wife because you've visited her social networking site just about a million times since you first discovered *he* has a page, thus realizing he's got a little wifey with a page as well. That was in the beginning though, when the shock was overwhelming and you just couldn't get past the fact that he'd done the one thing he'd sworn he would never do, get married again. Now it's only now and again that you visit her page, not even bothering with his. He doesn't update it anyway. As you're thinking of this you realize it has been a full month since you've even thought about him or his mousy little woman.

There you go being catty again, something Stella warned you about.

"There's no sense being mad at her," you hear Stella chide. *"She's done nothing to you."*

You wanted to yell at her that day. You wanted to tell her that, yes this girl has done something to you. She's married the guy you have loved since you were thirteen years old. She should be shot. Or maimed. Or just given a good talking to.

You take a sip of ice-cold mocha and try to turn your attentions back to your book, but it's no use.

What the hell is he doing in *your* favorite coffee shop? You're sure that there are rules against this sort of thing. Shouldn't one of you leave? And since he's always been the one that hates public, shouldn't it be him! You think you might just walk over there and ask him, but decide against it when your phone rings. You look down to see the name STELLA glaring out at you. Damn, does she have radar?

"Hello?" you answer.

"Hey, girl, where ya at?"

She's got some rap song blaring in the background and you hold the phone away from your ear to stop the assault. "Can you turn that down?" you quip.

She does.

"Now, what did you ask?"

"What're you doin?" she asks.

"Sipping coffee at Nan's, trying to read a book." You ponder whether or not you should tell her.

"Oh, I'm sorry. I didn't mean to bug ya," she says, trying not to sound hurt that you snipped at her, but you can tell that she is.

Feeling guilty, you decide to be honest. "It's not you," you say with a sigh. "Guess who I am staring at right now?"

There's silence.

"Well," you say. "Guess."

"I don't know," she says, but you can hear that caution in her tone.

"Ben," you say, raising your cup for another sip.

"Ben?" There's a pause. "You're not stalking him are you?"

Before you can stop it coffee is shooting out of your mouth, following your laughter. "No!" you screech. Grabbing the bunch of napkins you'd had the good sense to pick up, you dab at the drops of coffee currently staining your favorite vintage top. "Of course not!"

With a glance upward you see you've attracted the attention of almost everyone in the room, including your ex and his significant other. Though how she can be *that* significant you'll never know.

"Shit," you breathe.

"What?" Stella asks on the other end. She's got an edge in her voice.

"You made me spit coffee all over my favorite peasant top, number **one**," you quip. "And number two, he's seen me. Him and his mousy little wife."

"What's he doing?"

"What he always does. Just staring at me, like I'm some kind of sideshow freak!"

"Get out of there!" she yells. "Leave!"

"No!" you yell in a whisper. "I was here first and this is **my** favorite coffee shop!"

You try to turn your attention away and act as though you haven't seen him. He turns his attentions back to his wife, but she is still staring at you. Is it possible that she knows who you are?"

"What's happening?" Stella asks, practically screaming.

"I'm giving up on my top. You owe me one."

"I don't care about your top. You probably only paid three bucks for it anyway! What's happening with *him*!"

"He's talking to her, but she's staring at me." Your heart seizes as she stands up and begins to walk your way. "Oh my God, she's coming over here. What the hell!"

You can see why he's attracted to her. She's skinny and jerks like him always go for the skinny, although you were always curvaceous in high school, as were a couple of other of his girlfriends. You guess he's lost his sense of what's attractive because this girl is almost rail thin, no boobs, and small feet. Okay, maybe he doesn't care about her feet. Men are so easy when it comes to a skinny girl, as if that makes one interesting. You shift your size sixteen frame in the chair, trying to look as intimidating as possible.

"No she's not!" Stella gasps.

"Sure is."

You pretend not to notice her when she stops in front of you. Inside you're screaming *oh shit, oh shit, oh shit*, but outside you try to remain cool and calm.

"Excuse me," she says.

You look at her, then past her to him. His eyes are transfixed on the situation at hand, but he doesn't dare move.

Coward.

"Stell, hold on, k?" you say into the phone.

"Don't hang up!" Stella screams.

You laugh. "Just hold on." You look up at her. Her name is Julie, you know this because of the webpage, and you know that she has a one-year-old child with the man who used to be the boy you loved. You smile. "Yes?"

"Is your name Charlotte Edmonds?"

Damn, damn, damn!

"Yes," you say, maintaining your smile. Your mind is racing with thoughts, wondering what he may have told her about your relationship and hoping she's not gonna hit you. Mousy girls can fight too! "Have we met?"

"Um, no," she says. She looks back at Ben and you feel your stomach erupt again. "I'm sorry, my husband said I shouldn't bother you, but I just couldn't help myself."

Still wearing the smile, though it feels more than a little awkward at this time, you say, "You're no bother at all. How can I help you?"

"We kind of met last month. You came to the Arts Guild."

You remember the Arts Guild, but do not remember her being there.

"You spoke about your book, *25 Things Men Do Wrong.*"

You laugh and you can hear Stella laughing on the other end. "Y-yes, I remember speaking there, but I'm sorry I don't remember you."

"I came in late."

You laugh. "That explains it."

Something has happened. You're floating above your body, watching this bizzaro scene. Your first love's wife has come to speak to you about your book. This means he hasn't mentioned you to her at all.

"Have you purchased a copy?"

"Yes. My husband hates it." She laughs, a nervous kind of sputter, and you suddenly find yourself liking her a little more.

"Why would he hate it?"

She leans closer. "He says I am using it to grade him."

You laugh despite yourself and on the other end of the line you hear Stella howl. Your first love is married to a woman who purchased your book, and she uses it to tell him what he is doing wrong! It's the sweetest revenge!

"I'm sure he's overreacting." You can feel the sparkle in your eyes. You look over at Ben. He's fiddling with the lid to his cup, and his face has turned the same shade of copper as the mop on his head. You laugh again.

"It's specifically number 17," she continues, delightfully oblivious that she is making this the best day of your life.

"Number 17… Oh, number 17. Wow." You look at him again. He is mortified. You love it! "Well…" You want to tell her the book is all in good fun. Nothing to take too seriously, but you have been where she is. You have been with this man whose hands are better than the rest of him. Well, that and his kisses.

"Could you come and meet him?"

When the howling scream erupts from the phone you hit the little red end button. "I don't think so," you say.

"Oh. Not even for a moment? He's really angry with me, but if you speak to him…"

The devious part of you wants to say yes. That part wants to go over and gloat over him wallowing in his embarrassment. That devious part, you know, comes from years of making a fool out of yourself over him and being a laughingstock because you just couldn't get past him, but mostly it is from the foolishness you feel for having loved someone so much who'd never once loved you.

You look over at him once more and know that if you walk over to that table you will be that same sad girl that couldn't move forward. You'd still be that girl waiting by the phone for him to call back, or waiting on that email message after you'd found him online. It never came because he'd never cared enough for you to give you a second thought.

You smile at her. Leaning forward you cover her small hand with your own. "I am so glad you purchased my book," you say. "But I can't go over to that table. I can't go backward when I've already come so far."

She looks dumbfounded, and there's no reason why she shouldn't be. You wonder if she will tell him the puzzling words you've told her, but realize that it makes no difference. You are well removed from that sad little girl of your past.

"There's nothing there for me." You gather your belongings and stand up. She stands as well. "I'm sorry, but I have to go now," you tell her.

You don't look at him as you leave the coffee shop. There's no need. You know that she's already back at the table and he's chiding her for bothering you, but he still will not tell her that you used to be his girlfriend.

"Hey, sorry I'm late," a handsome blond man says, stepping in your path. "It took a little longer than expected."

You smile and say, "You're right on time." Gathering him up in your arms you kiss him. "Have I told you how much I love you lately?"

He looks suspicious. "Yes. Why?"

You laugh. "No reason."

He smiles. "Are you ready?"

"I just need to call Stella back and then we can go."

"I'm gonna step in and get me a beverage then."

You laugh at the exaggerated way he pronounces *beverage*, as you step off to the side and begin to dial the number.

"Well!" Stella answers after half a ring.

"She wanted to talk to me about my book," you giggle.

"I know! Number 17! I couldn't remember it, so I got the book out and looked it up!" She cackles. "I guess some things never change!"

You laugh. "I guess not. She wanted me to go and talk to him."

Stella's laughter stops suddenly. "Did you?"

"Nah," you say. "There's nothing there for me. Never was."

"I'm proud to hear you say that."

"Thanks. I'm kinda proud of me too." The door opens and she is joined once again by her beau. "Look, Stephen and I are going shopping. Can we stop by later?"

"Sure! See ya then!"

You slide your phone into the leather satchel, circa 1975, hanging off your waist, and look at Stephen. "What's up?" you ask as you begin your descent to the parking lot. Five steps count! "You look a little weirded out."

"Ben was in there."

"Really?" you say, chucking the remnants of your coffee in the bin. You link your arm to his and give him your best you-are-the-man-for-me smile. "I didn't notice."

Lips

Jenny tried to focus. The task was difficult enough, given the subject she was being forced to focus on, but the fact that she was staring at the most luscious pair of lips she'd ever seen was something else altogether.

She shifted in her chair, one of the hard ones the library insisted on having instead of providing the student body with something remotely comfortable to sit on. She pushed the mass of black bang away from her face, wishing she hadn't settled on the heavy bang look. Lorie Hensen would never dream of a heavy bang, and she has touched those lips. Grabbing her bag from the floor she fumbled until she found a long barrette. Within moments the confounded hair was out of her face, pinned back appropriately on her head, and she was looking right at those plump pink lips.

Why did she want to kiss them so badly?

"Are you okay?" the owner of the preoccupation asked.

Jenny smiled, dipping her head a bit to hide the blush. "Yes. Sorry. I shouldn't have gone with bangs. They're distracting."

A smile tugged at the corners of those beautiful lips, and soon a row of perfect white teeth were staring out at her. "I think your hair is cute."

"Thanks."

She met the green eyes that seemed to be searching for something.

"What?" she said, the heat creeping into her face again.

"I was thinking maybe we should call this quits for today. You've focused for a whole fifteen minutes and my mind isn't really on math anyway."

"Are you picking on me Daniel?" she quipped in fun. "Because I can focus for way longer than fifteen minutes."

He laughed. "Not at all. I just thought you might want to get out of here."

The butterflies in her tummy told her she most definitely did, but her mind said no in a hurry.

"I know this great spot I would like to show you."

"Sure," she said. Who could tell the cutest boy in school no?

His car was a Subaru Outback. She'd always pegged him as a corvette kind of guy, or a vintage muscle car kind. How did you peg a guy that is simultaneously a jock and a nerd? He kind of defied the traditional high school categories. He'd been voted best looking. She couldn't disagree.

Pulling out of the parking lot, they headed away from town and she knew where they would be going. She knew because it is where he took all of the girls he wanted to have his way with. There were enough stories going around that school about Danny Point that she didn't even listen anymore. Well, mostly.

And now he had chosen her.

How did something like that happen?

She was silent as they drove down the highway and then turned down a narrow one-lane gravel road just before the exit to the next town. As many stories as she had heard, she'd never known the exact location to Danny Point until this moment.

It was a long road. Dark and hazardous. Trees grew thick and branches reached out for the car as it passed, each of their spindly fingers seeming to brush the side of the sporty station wagon.

"You okay?" he asked, as they pulled to a stop in front of the man-made lake that originated with the housing development on the other side. It was, in fact, the same housing development Lorie Hensen lived in.

"Yes," she answered a little quicker than intended.

He switched off the ignition and crawled out of the driver seat. She followed him and soon they were both looking out over the lake. His brown hair moved with the breeze and those lips were pulled back in the softest smile.

She couldn't wait to taste them.

"What do you think?" he asked.

"It's beautiful on this side. Not so much on the other."

He laughed. "Agreed." He sat down, motioning for her to do the same. "I love this place."

"Why?"

"It's private, for one. I also like to think about what I'm gonna do next year when I'm outta here."

"Wouldn't you do that in private?"

He looked at her, confused.

"You bring a lot of girls here, Daniel."

He laughed. "You're right. But I also come here alone. A lot."

She decided she would bite. "So what're you going to do next year?"

"I've been accepted to a school in England."

"Are you serious?" She didn't believe it implicitly. She'd heard he was going to State. "That's fantastic."

"Yeah. It was."

"Was?"

He 'humphed'. "I know you've heard I'm going to State." She nodded.

"My parents can't afford to send me to that school in England. So I'm stuck here."

"I didn't know."

"Nobody knew," he said, his eyes fixed on the water before them. "Now you're the only one." He turned to look at her. "Can you keep my secret, Jenny?"

"Why does it need to be a secret?"

He shrugged. "I just need it to be. Are you good with that?"

"Yeah." She looked out over the water. "So what now?"

"What do you mean?" he asked, turning to her.

"I know why you bring girls out here," she whispered. "Are you going to use me now and then ignore me tomorrow?"

He turned her to face him, grasping her beneath the knees and turning her around on her bottom. He was strong.

She should have known that.

"No, I'm not going to use you." He released the barrette in her hair, smoothing the heavy bang across her forehead. "And I'm certainly not going to ignore you."

"So what are you going to do?" she asked.

He cupped her cheek, running his thumb over her burgundy-colored lips. "I'd really like to kiss you," he said, his voice deeper than she'd ever heard it before.

She lowered her knees, crossing them in the style that had once been called 'Indian'. "I'd really like to let you," she whispered.

Her mind screamed NO! He's lying you fool!

She knew that he was. Expected that he was.

But she wanted to use him just as much as he wanted to use her. His lips were her prize, and as he leaned closer she closed her eyes in anticipation of what they would feel like.

She was not disappointed.

Garland

She twisted, trying to right herself in the mangled mess that was the sheets. She'd purchased them specifically for this purpose. It was bad enough what they were doing. She didn't need, or want, to lower herself further by using sheets countless strangers had slept on (or goodness knows what else).

"Where are you going?" he asked, trying to pull her back down to him. "I'm just getting started."

She looked back at him. He wasn't what would be considered Mr. GQ. In fact, the other women in their circle would be shocked if they found out that the two of them had come together. Not because he was unattractive (she found him quite irresistible), but because he wasn't someone who might be considered popularly handsome.

Why could she never describe him without first saying that he is no Keanu Reeves or some other man that should be arrested for being so beautiful? It's not as if she was criminally beautiful.

"Hey," he said, his hand cupping her cheek. "Where'd you go?"

She laid her head to the side, turning her face to kiss his palm. "I was just trying to think of how to describe you," she answered.

"Bear," he said with no hesitation. "Describe me as a bear."

She laughed. "Really? Why a bear?"

"They're ravenous and so am I."

A high-pitched giggle escaped from between her swollen lips as he pretended to attack her. She stopped when he paused and looked at her. His expression had gone from mischievous to serious.

"Do you want to know how I would describe you?"

She didn't. She couldn't. There was too much risk. If he described her as anything less than beautiful she might be devastated and if he described her as such she might be equally destroyed. Pulling away from him, she jumped out of the bed.

"Where are you going?"

She turned back to him, giving him a sultry yet mischievous smile. At least she hoped that was what it looked like. Grabbing the shopping bag that would help to provide her alibi for the night she went into the bathroom and pushed the door almost closed.

"What's in the bag?" he asked. She loved hearing that bit of deviousness in his gruff voice.

"I had to pick up a few things for tomorrow. We're going to the parents for dinner."

"Ah," he said. "I'm doing the same thing." There was a pause and then, "come on, woman. I want to devour you one more time before we have to leave."

She stuck her head through the crack in the door. "You are so impatient."

"Only with you."

"Liar," she said with a laugh. "Close your eyes. I have a gift for you."

He did as she instructed. Opening the door she stepped out into the sparsely lit room. She had no idea why she'd decided to do just what she'd done. Who was she kidding? It was all about maintaining the precious balance and precarious position they both found themselves in. One false move, such as becoming *too* involved could make their entire house of cards collapse. That was something she was not ready to face.

"You can open them now," she whispered.

He took the sight of her in. Never before had she stood in front of a man wearing nothing more than Christmas garland. There was something forbidden about it, and she couldn't help feeling that she was putting some sort of blemish on the holiday by using trimming for her home as lingerie.

Somehow it didn't matter.

"Wow," he said, his blue eyes twinkling bright. "This is my favorite gift so far."

He stood up, his nakedness glowing in the dim light of dime store lamps. Slowly, he approached and she closed her eyes as he stepped up behind her.

"Don't rip it," she breathed, as he placed one hand on each of her shoulders.

"Oh, don't worry," he whispered, his warm breath tickling her ear. "I'm going to unwrap you slowly."

****

She opened her eyes when the buzzing coming from beside her did not subside. She grabbed the device, and slid out of her lover's arms, making her way to the bathroom. Quietly, she pushed the door to and turned the lock.

"Hello?"

"Hey, where are you?"

She raked a shaking hand through her disheveled hair. "Wh-at do you mean? I told you I was staying with my sister tonight."

"I called Maddy and she said she hadn't seen you yet. It's after ten. Where are you?"

"Why are you questioning me, Bryan?"

"Because you're not where you said you would be, Liz. This is not the first time you haven't been where you said you would be."

It would have been easy to tell him the truth just then. She knew that it would have brought a measure of peace to her, but she couldn't help thinking what it would do to Bryan. She loved him. Instead she said, "I had some last minute shopping to do."

"Liz,"

"I have to go, Bryan. I'll see you tomorrow." She stood up, observing her soft form in the mirror. Here was the image of an unfaithful wife. A liar. As always she found herself hating that reflection. Each time she swore she would never do it again. Bryan is a good husband. He is available and sweet. He is honest and caring. Most of all he still loved her after fifteen years of marriage.

She would go into the room and tell him right now. She would say that this has been some huge mistake and then she would tell him that they can never see one another in this capacity again, but even as she began to pull her sweater dress over her shoulders she knew she wouldn't. The thought of telling Bryan of her indiscretion made her physically ill, but the thought of never being touched by the man in the adjoining room again made every inch of her ache. Inside and out.

"Was that Bryan?" he asked when she opened the door to rejoin him. He was propped up on one elbow.

She nodded.

"I don't want to ask what he wanted, but I really do."

She managed a semi-laugh. "I told him I was spending the night with my sister. He called her to check up on me and she told him she hadn't seen me." Grabbing her hair tie from the floor she wrapped it around the bun she'd managed to form in the center of her auburn clad head.

"So he doesn't trust you?"

She looked at him. "Would you?" Perching on the side of the bed she began pulling her fur-lined boots on. "If you caught Kim in countless lies would you trust her?"

He didn't answer.

She turned to him, her still-naked foot dangling from the bed. "What would you do if you thought Kim was having an affair?"

He stood up, grabbing his pants from the floor.

"Well? What would you do, James?" She asked, shoving her foot into the awaiting boot. When he didn't answer she stood and walked over to him, forcing him to meet her gaze. "What would you do if the woman you can't seem to leave was sleeping with another man?"

"You never asked me to leave her."

She shook her head, turning her blurring eyes from him. "That's not the point," she said, her voice wavering. Stooping, she grabbed the discarded garland from the hotel room floor. "I have to go."

He grabbed her, forcing her to look at him. "Liz,"

"Stop," she sobbed. "Just let me go."

"I can't." She tried to pull away, but he held tight to her. "Dammit, Liz, talk to me. What do you want?"

She looked at him, embarrassed that she'd allowed her emotions to get the best of her. She blamed Bryan. If he hadn't called she wouldn't have been forced to confront the adulterous heathen in the mirror. "I- I." She looked down, unable to tell him she had long ago crossed over from the realm of lust into something more. It wasn't love. Could it be? No, they didn't know one another well enough for that.

How strange that they could know so little about one another yet so much. She knew every inch of his body and he every inch of hers, but she couldn't even begin to answer what his favorite color might be or what he dreamed of being as a child.

Bryan wanted to be a police officer. What did James want to be?

"What are you saying?" he asked.

She shook her head, her eyes meeting the deep blue pools of concern staring back at her. "I'm saying that I have to go." Raising up on her toes, she pressed her lips to his allowing the heat to fill her up again. "Merry Christmas," she whispered when they parted. "I hope you liked your gift."

"I thoroughly enjoyed my gift," he said with a devilish grin, but she could still see the worry in his gaze. "Do I get to keep the garland?"

"Nope. But you do get to keep the memories."

Rain

Louisa had been cooped up for days. Even now she was curled up on the window seat of the parlor, her eyes peering out into the gray evening searching for a break in the clouds that she knew wasn't there, just waiting for her moment to get out. To get away.

"Louisa, come away from there." her husband said from his place by the fire. "Come warm yourself by the fire."

She looked over at him. Frederick was fourteen years her senior. He was tall, thin, and his nose seemed to protrude from his face in such a fashion that she might hang a scarf from it. In fact, she had often imagined doing just that. Anything to cover up those thin lips that he was always trying to press to her skin. It was a circumstance she'd never wanted.

"I like to watch the rain," she said, trying to muster a smile.

Truth was, she was willing the rain to depart. For weeks she'd been contemplating an escape from Frederick, but this rain was serving only to aid in her imprisonment. If it would just clear up she could go for a turn in the garden and just keep turning until she landed some place far from here. Far from Frederick.

"Darling," he said, rising.

She watched his tall lanky frame cross the divide between them quickly, and her panic began to rise. She'd managed to feign some type of illness most every time her husband had threatened intimacy during their seven-month marriage, but her excuses were becoming flimsy. Either that or he had ceased to care about her trifles.

She pulled the wedding quilt tighter about her. Its vivid reds and yellows were a stark contrast to the surrounding gloom. They served to remind her that she had once been happy, and she had once been part of a family that exuded brightness and happiness.

"Darling, what's the matter?" he asked, sitting beside her, sliding his arm around her shoulders. She resisted the urge to shrug him away. "Louisa, my dearest, please tell me how I can make you smile again."

She wanted to scream, "*Let me go! I'll be happy if I can just go home!*" but she remained quiet.

"How about," he said with an exaggerated pause. "We go for a carriage ride." Then he looked out the window and laughed. "Perhaps not. Don't want my darling wife to catch cold." He pressed his forefinger to her nose and chuckled. Then, his pointed face growing serious, he began to trail his finger along the edge of the quilt, trying to playfully free it from her grasp. "Perhaps we could..."

A panic seized her as he tried, a little too forcefully, to pry her fingers away from the only thing protecting her from his touch. How could she stop this nightmare?

"My sister!" she shouted, jumping up from the seat to put as much distance between them as possible. "I would be most pleased if you were to go and fetch my sister."

His face held uncertainty. "But the weather is not suitable for travel at this time, my love," he said, his head jerking toward the rain splattered pane.

Of course she'd known he wouldn't want to go in this kind of weather, but she was so desperate to be free of him; if only for a few hours while he traveled to get her sister and return. She put on her best pout. He liked her pout. At least he had when they'd married. He'd said she was like a sweet puppy with big sad eyes. The smile that spread along her thin lips was revolting.

He stood, walking over to her, his arms outstretched. "Of course you would, my dear." He held her to him, stroking the length of her hair. "I promise to fetch her as soon as the weather breaks."

She pulled away, allowing the quilt to pool at her feet. He loved her silhouette in the lavender silk and lace dress she'd worn for supper, and at this point she was willing to do almost anything to get him out, even allowing him to devour her with his vulture like eyes. "Frederick, please. You know that my sister brings me joy." She smiled. "Please, darling."

He considered her plea, his eyes going first to the rain soaked windowpane and then to the glowing fire. She knew he was contemplating what sort of reward he would get for fetching her sister in such weather. Surely he could have the driver sit out in the rain and he could be in the carriage, but she knew that wasn't likely to happen. Her husband, if he was nothing else, was very proud and would carry out this task alone.

It was cruel for her to ask that he go out into such weather, but another hour in his presence might send her to the roof where she could plunge into the sweet oblivion of the hereafter. At least there she would be free of him.

How could she ever have agreed to marry him?

"Of course," he said gathering her up in his long arms. He was like a spider, and she was the fly caught in his web, trying desperately to get out. "What kind of husband would I be if I didn't go fetch your sister?"

"Really?" she asked, stunned that he was entertaining her request.

He pressed his mouth to hers, holding her with one hand on each arm. "Of course!" he exclaimed when he released her. "If your sister will drive away your melancholy I will fetch her. I will ring for Jessie to get the buggy ready and I will go at once."

She smiled, thinking for the flash of a moment that she might be able to love him. "Thank you, Frederick."

****

Louisa stretched out like a cat waking from a luxurious nap. Perhaps in a way she was like that cat. She hadn't slept so sound in a long while. Many nights were spent listening for Frederick, wondering if he would sneak in to make her perform her duties as wife. The fact that it was morning might have gone unnoticed, were it not for Harriet entering with her breakfast tray.

This was the reason, she thought as she situated herself at the small breakfast table that had been pulled closer to the hearth. For comfort she had given up herself. Her mother had assured her that it would be okay, that she would grow to love Frederick and be able to tolerate his affections, but even now she knew that was untrue. She smiled at Harriet, but inside she continued to sob.

"Did Frederick have his breakfast, Harriet?" she asked absently as she watched the rain trickle down the glass east-facing windows. On a bright sunny day they served to bring light into her dreary room and life. There would be no cheer today.

"No, ma'am," the young girl said, her tight red curls bouncing under her white cap as she illustrated her answer.

"Why on earth not?"

"He's not here."

Louisa's head snapped away from the windows. "Not here?"

"No, ma'am, he hasn't returned from his trip."

Louisa placed her bread on the gold-trimmed plate. "Bring me my... No, I must get dressed."

"But..."

"Get a gown, Harriet. Hurry! I'll wear the purple one today. Yes, the one with the lace." She grabbed the frock from the young girl. "Go and fetch Jessie. Now!"

After Louisa dressed she made her way downstairs. Harriet had called for Jessie, as she had been instructed, and he was waiting by the back door.

"Ride out and try to find Frederick please, Jessie," Louisa instructed. "He went to fetch my sister." Her heart clinched as she thought of her sister stranded with her husband. How could she have left her with him?

Jessie nodded, his gray eyes as solemn as the perpetual mood of the house.

"Harriet, I will be in my room," Louisa said, her hands fidgeting with the lace-trimmed handkerchief she'd already twisted into a deformed mass. She climbed the stairs, her heart heavy. Frederick had not returned. Surely something had happened to him. He wouldn't have left her alone. Not when he was so sure that he would be rewarded so handsomely for his sacrifice. But what if nothing had happened? What if her sister had met with an unhappy circumstance when he'd picked her up? What if he had... No, she couldn't think of her sister being so ill-used.

Unable to do anything more, Louisa made her way to the rocking chair situated at the window facing out toward the road. Being on the second floor it afforded a clear view of the world below.

When she thought she might burst from fear and anxiety, she spied a man walking beside a horse on the horizon. She knew Jessie and his lop-sided walk when she saw him. Her heart pounding, she gathered her skirts and tore down the stairs to meet him.

Throwing the door open, she rushed across the portico and out to where Jessie stood beside his steed, his face streaked with tears. "I wuz too late, Miss Louisa," he sobbed. "I'm so sorry."

Breathless and frantic she asked, "Is my sister..." She took a deep breath. "Jessie, I cannot look. Is she there?"

He shook his head and she breathed a sigh of relief. "And Frederick?"

He bowed his head.

With quaking legs Louisa made her way over to the buggy hitched to Jessie's horse. There, laid out in his riding clothes, was the lifeless body of her husband. His brown hair, thinning on top, was plastered to his ghostly face. The thin lips that looked grotesque in life were gray and spread into a grim line.

"I'm sorry, Miss," Jessie said. "He musta misjudged the road and overturned the carriage. Harriet's gone to get the doc, but I don't know what good he's gonna do." She looked at him and he sobbed. "I shoulda stopped him. I'm so sorry, Miss." After a few moments of shameful sobbing Jessie stopped. He looked at her, this woman who seemed stunned to silence. "Miss Louisa, are you alright? Do you need to sit down?" She didn't answer and the older man grew more concerned. "Ain't you gonna say something?"

A slight smile tugged at the corners of her mouth and he feared she was going mad. She turned her bright green eyes on him and said, "When did it stop raining?"

Ex

When Lorna called to tell me she'd run into my ex I hadn't believed her. After all, the last time I ran into him (not literally of course. Well, maybe...) he'd mentioned something about moving out of the country. From that moment I became resigned to the fact that I would never see him again.

"You're not serious," I said into the blue-tooth permanently glued to my ear.

"I am totally serious," she said.

I wanted to ask a million questions, the first being *"where does he live?"* But I refrained. It was hard to do, and something told me that Lorna knew that, the way she prattled on and on about this man that I had been accused of stalking (not true) for more than ten years. Did it really count as stalking if you visited his social networking page three or four times a day waiting for an update.

"I thought he'd moved to Puerto Rico," I said.

Lorna laughed, a loud cackling sound. "No, honey," she said as if I were a four year old trying to get at something I shouldn't. "He has been right here the entire time. Just flying under the radar. At least that's what he said."

I knew what she was getting at. She might as well have said *He's just been hiding from you, Anni.*

"Well, that's nice then. And he's doing well?"

"He's doing fabulous!" she gushed. "And," she paused for effect. "He's *single*!"

I guess I shouldn't have been surprised to feel that nagging, the one I thought I had moved on from. I tell you what, my friends, you don't know shame until you're stuck on one guy for way longer than need be. The *really* sad fact was that he had never been that into me and it took a lot of years to get it.

"Anni, you still there?"

"Yup," I said. "But I've got to go."

There was a chuckle on the other end. "Off to the internet, I guess?"

"What?"

"He's not a big internet person. That was his ex."

"Lorna, please give me a little credit. I've got a lunch appointment."

There was another chuckle and I contemplated walking over to her office building to give her a good smack. If she was any kind of friend what so ever she wouldn't have even mentioned him. She knew that I was still having issues getting over him. Then again, Lorna had never really been any kind of friend.

****

"If she was your friend at all she wouldn't have called you, Anni," my best friend of forever, Piper, said over lunch.

Yes, she was my appointment.

"Why did she do it then?" I asked, taking an angry bite of my hot dog.

Today we'd decided to meet at a local hot dog place. The best in the city.

"Who knows. Lorna has her own agendas and she doesn't care who she hurts with them."

"She invited me to dinner tonight."

Dr. Pepper and ice spewed across the wrought iron table. I grabbed a paper napkin from beside my dog tray and began to dab the dark liquid away from my face.

"Sorry," she offered.

"Yeah." She sat upright in her chair, her green eyes fixed on my face. I knew what she expected, but still I said, "What!"

"You're going, aren't you?"

"I was invited," I said a little too quickly.

"It is astounding to me the mess you will go through just to get the scoop on him!"

I bowed my head, waiting for the fresh shame to pass. "I am not going to talk about him. I am just going to dinner with Lorna."

"Anni, you can lie to everyone else, and maybe they will believe you, but you can't lie to me. You don't need to go."

I didn't raise my head.

"Dammit, Anni!" she said, smacking the table.

My head snapped up.

"You don't need to go," she repeated. "You've come so far. I don't want to see you go this way again."

"It's fine," I assured her. "I'm not going any way. I don't even think about him anymore."

It was a lie. And that was precisely why scarcely an hour later I was on the internet trying to find out as much information as possible about the ex that should have never shown back up. I had just stumbled upon a great site that might possibly give me some answers when the door to my office opened.

"You've got a call on line three, Anni," my sometimes assistant, Toni, said. She was too cute for words, and I hated her for it, but not in a bad way. She couldn't help it she was born disgustingly beautiful.

"Thanks." I smoothed out my hair (don't ask me why), took a deep breath, and picked up the line. ""This is Anni," I said with confidence.

"Anni, darling," Lorna said, her tone high and flighty. "Tonight at eight. Monticello's."

I agreed and replaced the receiver on its cradle. For the life of me I couldn't understand why Lorna, someone I talked to maybe once a year, had now made a second appearance in one day.

Eight o'clock.

But did I care? Piper was right, I really have come a long way. I scarcely thought of him now, and I only checked on his social sites every now and then. Maybe once a week if I have to get specific, but there was something inside that made me want to go. If Lorna knew something about him I wanted to know.

And, yes, I do know how ridiculous that is.

****

It was seven fifty-five and I was standing outside of the priciest restaurant in town. I contemplated going inside once more. Not only was I hesitant because of the price (one meal could potentially set me back half a week's pay. Maybe a quarter), but also because I didn't want to confirm what Lorna thought she knew about me.

She didn't know me. And she certainly had no idea of my feelings for the man I had once envisioned as my husband.

I walked to the wall of windows that lined the dining room, looking for the shock of red hair that would signal Lorna's presence. I found her at a table in the center of the room. How fitting for her, I thought.

Her hair was pulled into a tight bun and her lips were the deepest burgundy I had ever seen. She was wearing a black dress with a waterfall bodice that fell in all the right places to accentuate her bust line. I suddenly remembered why I never saw Lorna more than twice a year. She was a skeez.

She threw her head back, her deep red lips opening to illustrate her laugh, her hand stretching out toward her companion.

I guess I shouldn't have been surprised to see my ex sitting across from her looking as handsome as ever, but I was.

Yearning

If I asked you what it is you yearn for above all else what do you think you would answer? I asked my sister and she kind of looked at me like most seven year olds do when you stump them. It was like I had asked her an unanswerable question.

Maybe it is.

Even now, twenty years later, I am not sure that I even know.

The funny thing is, my sister knows it. She's Twenty-seven years old and she has answered the question that I cannot even begin to ponder.

Does this count as pondering?

"Hey," comes a voice out of the void.

At first it seems as though I am imagining it, but then I know that it's my partner, Mickey. We chose not to get married because the whole marriage thing seems so blasé. We talked about it once and all it did was make me feel like I was attempting to play grown up in a world that I will never belong to. He says it's just another of my hang ups, but I know my limitations.

I turn my head to him as he leans in to give me a kiss. After six years his kiss can still ignite in me a flame bright enough to light up the darkest sky. "Hey," I whisper.

"Have you been crying?" He touches my damp cheek and, as always, I dip my head in embarrassment. "What's wrong?"

"It's just this article. I can't seem to get it right. I want to show the world that I have something important to say, but I can't make it come out." I sigh. I know he is worried, his gaze tells me that. He is always so quiet when he thinks there's something wrong with me.

Maybe he should be.

I lean into him and he wraps his long arms around me. "Why do you worry about the whole world when you write?"

"I don't know," I sulk. "I just want the world to read what I write, but at the same time I am paralyzed by this fear that they might."

He chuckled. "You are so complicated my little Nikita."

My name is Nikki, but for some reason he has always called me his little Nikita and I have never protested. I like that he has a name that is for only me.

"So what's wrong with this one?" he asked, sliding his large hands up and down my arms.

"I just feel like I'm spinning my wheels."

"What's it about?"

"Me. Jenni. Absolute truth."

He laughed. "No truth is absolute, babe. You know that."

"I know."

I pulled away from him. Standing up, I paced back and forth from the red futon we had been using as a sofa for three years to the large window that looked out over the lake. Most days it was the home of my dreams, offering me seclusion and quiet, but today all it did was show me how alone I was in this world. No wonder I was holding so tightly to Mickey.

He was behind me, his slight frame towering above me. His arms were around my waist. "Tell me what you want to say," he whispered.

We stood like that, both of us staring out into the late afternoon, for what seemed like eternity. What did I want to say? What did I feel like I needed to say with this particular story? It was about my sister and I. Our lives. No. Not really about our lives at all. Not per say.

I retreated into myself, pulling away from my love and going over to the small table that served as my desk. With a thud I sat.

He was behind me again, his hands running along my arms. He leaned down and his warm breath tickled my ear as he said, "Ask me."

"Ask you what?"

"Your question."

I smiled, turning around to face him. He crouched down, his full lips pulling back into a crooked grin, and his brown eyes sparkling. This was why I loved him so. He was my muse in the flesh. I raked my fingers through his raven hair, tugging at the strands that curled inward at the base of his neck. "What is it you yearn for above all else?"

"For the world to hear your words."

My smile broadened, as he knew it would. His answer is all I'd been yearning for since childhood. Twenty years later I was still terrified to admit that I wasn't born for what many women feel they are born for- to get married and have a family, though I wouldn't mind having a child someday. The reason for my creation was simply to tell stories to the world around me. The entire world.

He stood up, kissing my forehead. He wore a proud smile. "But they never will if you don't write." And with that he turned on his bare heels and made his exit.

It was the same tactic he used each time I felt lost. I stared after him until I could no longer hear the sound of his feet on the mahogany-colored hardwoods, and then I turned back to my computer, my confidence renewed.

If I asked you what it is you yearn for above all else what do you think you would answer?

Lament

Cynthia Sparks stood, her arms crossed tightly about her, in the falling snow. Before her the earth opened up, ready to swallow the gold-accented box perched above it. She looked around at the sparse number of people in attendance and thought it suited the man forever packed away in his fine prison.

The tall man adorned in black from the hat atop his head to the very tip of his patent leather toes looked at her. "Are we ready to begin?" he asked.

He was a walking cliché. How she had managed to find him she might never know. She looked at the box. Perhaps she hadn't found him at all. The deceased had always been a fan of the macabre. The fact that this priest looked as though he'd stepped out of a B-horror movie would have only thrilled Walter.

Her hand shot to her throat. She'd never intended to even *think* of his name again.

"Ma'am," the ghost masquerading as a preacher said, his long hand reaching out for her.

She recoiled, holding a hand up to let him know she was okay. "Go ahead," she managed through her tears.

"It's okay, Mom," her youngest son said, sliding an arm around her shoulders.

If only she could tell him that she knew it would be okay. Now everything would be okay. And the reason was because his father was lying in the box that the earth was waiting to cradle in its depths forever.

"I know," she said, patting his young hand. How did you tell a twenty year old that his father was a deliberately cruel man that you were happy to see dead? How did you even think such a thing? "I know."

When the man in the black hat finished his mini sermon, something her late husband would have loved, the attendants departed, leaving Cynthia and her son standing alone. He squeezed her shoulders. "Come on, Mom, let's get in out of this cold."

"I just need a few minutes," she said, patting his gloved hand. "You get Carol and the girls and go wait. I'll be there directly."

"You sure?"

She nodded. "I just want to say goodbye."

He released her, going to join his wife and their small twin girls. She watched as they made their way through the snow to the car awaiting them on the edge of the lawn. Cynthia waited until they'd climbed inside before turning back to where her husband now lay.

"I think you can hear me," she said, then laughed. "Of course you can hear me. You always promised I would never be free of you." She swatted at the tears that had begun to fall. "I won't mourn you," she said to that box topped with the largest arrangement of carnations she could find. They were his least favorite flower. He'd spent his life spiting her. This was her one show of defiance. Well, the first of two. This was the second. "I could never mourn a man who spent twenty years running around on me, having children with other women, and beating me when the mood struck. I thought I hated you for a long time, but it turns out I just hated myself. You thought you killed my spirit. Maybe you did for a while. I will not lament your absence in my life. I am free from your tyranny and your hypocrisies. " She laughed, throwing her head back to break the silence the blanket of snow had spread across her little corner of the earth. "I'm Free!"

She looked at the two men waiting to cover the casket with their large back hoe and smiled. "I'm free," she repeated this time more quietly. They didn't respond to her words, but they didn't need to. This was not their moment. This one belonged solely to her.

Stepping closer to the hole now surrounding her former husband, she pulled off the band that had kept her chained to him for so long and dropped it. With a clang it fell onto the box that was now covered with a thin dusting of snow and Cynthia Sparks walked away.

Moon

The parlor was quiet. She thought there would be some sound. She hadn't expected for it to be so utterly quiet. She stepped up to the pocket doors that had been closed to keep guests from wandering in before it was quite time. This was a difficult time for the adults in the house to be sure. She hadn't seen much of her mother for days, and her brother hadn't bothered to come out of his room since coming back from college three days earlier.

She touched the brass ring. One tug would open up the quiet room and allow life back in. This was the second wake they'd had in her home that she could remember. Most of the time two little boys came in and would sit with the body while everyone else in the house slept, but this time they hadn't been invited. She guessed it was because of the person lying so quietly behind those doors.

"Moon, honey," Loretta, the head housekeeper, said in a voice as soft as a mid-summer breeze. "You don't need to go in there." She slid a plump arm around the girl, pulling her close. "Why don't you come into the kitchen, little bit, we'll get you a glass of milk and some cookies."

Moon nodded, but she wasn't really sure why everyone continued to treat her as if something were terribly wrong. Except for the person in the parlor it was just like any other day. She allowed Loretta to lead her into the kitchen and plop her down at the small table with one cookie and a half glass of milk.

"There you go, sweetness," she said. "Now you go on out to play after you finish up and stay away from the parlor. You're momma will pitch a fit if you go in there."

"Yes, ma'am," she said, taking a nibble of the cookie. "Thank you." Then, before the aging housekeeper could leave her she asked, "Who's in there, Loretta?"

Loretta shook her head, her hand raising to her mouth to stifle the odd sound that still managed to escape. "You eat your cookie and go outside to play, okay?"

Moon nodded, but she sure did wish someone would tell her what was going on.

****

"Moon!"

She jerked her hand back from the brass ring, turning to face the owner of the shrill voice calling from the stairs.

"Moon Daniels, you come here right this moment!"

She walked over to the stairs, her head down. Her mother always had a way of doing that to her, making her feel as if she'd done something wrong even when she'd done nothing at all. She walked up the open stairs to the landing where her mother was waiting. She was wearing her black dressing gown and her long brown hair was wrapped up in a black silk turban. She looked sleek and sophisticated.

"What do you think you're doing at that door, young lady?" her mother snipped. "And look at your dress!"

Moon looked down at the dust on the front of her dress. She hadn't meant to fall into the dirt, but Buddy had pushed her.

"Now you will need a bath and a new dress! How could you do this?" She moaned. "How could you do this today?"

She watched as the older version of herself crumbled to the floor. "I didn't mean too, momma," she said.

Loretta rushed up the stairs, gathering the elder Daniels up and leading her away to her rooms. Moon stood on the landing watching after them, not knowing exactly what to do. It seemed she was either in the way or doing something wrong, no matter how good she tried to be.

"Come on, sweetie," Grenadine, the youngest of the house maids said. "Let's get you cleaned up."

For the second time she was allowing herself to be led away. It was strange, to say the least, that she would not be allowed to go into the parlor. Her mother always allowed her to before. In fact, she recommended it in order for her to become familiar with death. There was nothing worse than a child making a scene when introducing them to the situation beforehand could have prevented it. At least that was what her momma always said.

Grenadine laid her mourning dress across the bed and set to helping her off with the ruined pink summer gown she'd been dressed in that morning. "Now, you won't be able to go back outside to play after this," the young woman was saying. You've got to be a good girl. This is a hard time for your momma." She swiped the wash cloth across Moon's nose. "Can you do that for me?"

Moon nodded.

"You promise?"

Moon nodded her head again, her dark hair swinging back and forth.

"That's a good girl." Pulling her over to the bed, she slid the dress over Moon's head and smoothed it over her tiny frame. "This day's gonna be a hard one, peanut," she said as she worked to straighten the gown. "But you gotta hold onto your family. Okay?"

Moon nodded her head once more and Grenadine kissed the tip of her nose.

"I want you to go downstairs and sit with the rest of the guests, but you stay away from that parlor."

"But,"

"What?"

"Grenadine, who is in there? No one has told me and momma is so sad."

Her eyes became like glass and she took a deep breath. "Come here," she said, pulling Moon close. "Please just know that I am so sorry and that everything will be okay." She held the confused girl out at arm's length. "Okay?"

Moon nodded.

Grenadine kept staring at her, her hands remaining on her arms. There was something there that Moon didn't quite understand. She looked so terribly sad and her eyes were full of water.

"Why are you so sad?" Moon whispered, wiping away a tear that slid down the woman's cheek.

"It's a very sad day, baby," she said. "I'm just so sad for you. You go on now, sweetie," she said releasing her. "And be a good girl."

Moon ambled down the stairs, taking her seat on the small stool by the fireplace. There were already a lot of people surrounding her, all talking in hushed tones. What were they saying, she wondered? Did they know who was behind that door? And if they knew why couldn't she?

She thought she might be able to hear if she stayed really still and quiet, but she had been that way already and she hadn't heard. It might be due to the fact that everyone stopped talking when she appeared to be listening.

They were all much older than her. She knew most of them as her father's friends and business cohorts. At least that is what her mother called them.

"Hey, little Moon," Alexander Thompkins said, stopping in front of her. He was old. His belly was round and his hair, what was left of it, was white with some black here and there. He dressed very nicely, but the last button of his vest had popped off. She imagined it was from the vastness of his belly.

She smiled and he nodded, turning when the guests began to mutter and turn toward the staircase. There, standing regal at the bottom though her eyes were red and puffy, was Moon's mother. She was beautiful for a woman of her age. She'd been thirty-six when she'd given birth to her youngest ten years before and forty-five when she'd become a widow. Now she was standing in mourning clothes once more, looking as if she might collapse.

"Moon," she said, holding her hand out.

The child went to her mother's side immediately.

"Friends," her mother said, grasping tightly to her hand. "Thank you for coming. Moon and I will enter first and then you will join us. I cannot tell you how much it means to have your support at a time like this." Together they stepped up to the doors and her mother pulled the brass ring Moon had been lingering by all afternoon.

Her tiny heart began to pound as the heavy mahogany opened exposing the room she'd seen a million times. She held her momma back and began to shake her head. "I don't want to go in," she whispered.

Her mother held tighter to her hand and kept moving forward. "It's okay, Moon," she said.

Something was different this time. Whoever was waiting for them at the end of the long aisle was not someone that she wanted to see. You have to be prepared for these things. That's what her momma always said. She was very good at preparing someone for the worst. When her father had died Moon had known that he would do so and her mother had made sure that she was ready to see him lying so still.

"I don't want to see," she said, her breathing becoming shallow. "I don't know who it is." As they neared the casket she tried to free her hand from that of her mother's. "I'm not ready," she cried. "I don't know who it is."

Her mother stopped, pulling her into a crushing hug. "It's okay, Little Moon," she sobbed. "I know it's difficult, but you must pull yourself together." Releasing her embrace she pulled her young child the rest of the way down the aisle.

Moon couldn't remember how to move. She stood there, staring down at the lifeless body of her brother, holding tightly to her mother's hand.

"He was coming home from school," her mother said through her sobs. "He was mugged in town by some hooligans and they stabbed him."

Moon shook her head. "No," she said, suddenly remembering how to speak. "No, Mommy."

"I'm so sorry, my darling," she sobbed.

"He's in his room. He's not dead. He's not sick. Only sick people die." Moon dropped her mother's hand. "He's not sick," she repeated.

"Moon," her mother said, grabbing for her hand.

"You said only sick people die, Mommy. He's not sick. He's...."

Her mother wrapped her up in her arms. "I know, my darling. I know."

Moon tried to grab for her mother, but the room was getting dark. Her mother was no longer there. "Mommy!" she cried. "Mommy!" The parlor fell away and she began to drift.

"Hey, little bit," she heard a muddled voice say. "Come on over here and let's play." She opened her eyes, happy to find that she was outside. There was no parlor. No corpse that used to be her brother. She sat up, looking across the yard to where her brother was playing with their dog Sparky. He motioned for her to join him. "Come on, Moon!" he shouted.

She ran into his arms. "Momma told me you were dead, but I knew she was wrong. I just knew!"

He smiled, smoothing her hair back. "Let's not worry about that just now." He handed her the ball. "Here, it's your turn."

****

Loretta sat by the bedside of her mistress, trying desperately to keep her hands busy. She'd been crocheting since twilight. Finally the door opened and Doctor Lummox entered the room. She met him at the end of the bed.

"What happened?" she asked the doctor.

"Her little heart just gave out," he said, his eyes falling on the older woman lying unconscious in the bed, the curtains drawn around her. "It must have been the shock of seeing her brother." He looked at Loretta. "Did her mother really keep it from her?"

"Yes, sir. I think she thought it would be best." She choked out a sob. "What is she gonna do now?"

Curiosity

Lena peeked around the corner, making sure to remain hidden behind the large stack of boxes she'd discovered the night before. It was wrong, she knew, to spy on people. Especially during intimate moments such as this. Some things outsiders are just not supposed to know. At least that's what her mother had always told her, but she was almost grown now, and besides, this was Aunt Mona. She'd never had a real secret in her whole life. Not that thirty years was a long time.

"I know," Mona was saying into the glowing mobile phone raised to her ear. "Not yet. No. I…" She paused, her eyes darting around, checking her surroundings for anyone who might be listening.

Lena shrank back against the boxes. If Mona caught her she'd get a whipping for sure. Not that she'd had one for a while. Well, if you didn't count the one she'd gotten for spying on her big brother it had been a full three years. Who ever heard of a seventeen year old getting a whipping anyway?

Mona held the phone closer, cupping her hand over her bright red lips. Lena strained to hear what she might be whispering, but all she could make out was one word… "Soon."

"Where have you been?" Her momma asked when she allowed the screen door to slam closed behind her.

Their house could be one of those from an old magazine. Her mom sure did strive to make it look like it was a place from the old days instead of something that belonged in the twenty-first century. Her grandma said it belonged in the 1930s, but Lena's momma wouldn't hear anything against it. She said it was her house and she'd have it the way she wanted it.

"Around," Lena answered, trying her best to slip past her in the large foyer to get up the stairs and to the safety of her room. It was impossible to keep lying to her.

She seemed to have decided it wasn't worth it after contemplating pressing the issue, because instead of questioning her further about her whereabouts this afternoon she said, "That boy was here asking after you."

"What boy?" Lena turned her head too fast, her dirty blond hair (uncombed) swishing back and forth from the momentum.

Her momma leaned up against the banister, her pretty oval face all lit up with mischief. "What boy do you think?"

Their hair was the same, only her momma didn't keep it long anymore. She had it cut real short with a side bang that fell to the right side of her head. She wore some kind of hair wax to keep it looking svelte and polished. Svelte, that's the word her momma always used. Their body frames were the same too; only Lena didn't have the extra thirty pounds that children and age deliver to a woman.

"What do I care," Lena quipped with a smile. "He's just some silly boy."

"I didn't think Danny was just any boy," her momma teased. "I thought he was *the* boy."

"Danny?" Lena shook her head a little. "Danny?" she repeated, not believing it, even as it registered. "Danny, really?"

Her momma shook her head.

Lena jumped off the stairs, grabbing her mother's hands and jumping around. "Danny! Danny!"

"Yes, darlin, and he's comin back tonight to have supper with us, so you'd better go and make yourself presentable."

"Did he say why? I mean, I've wanted him to... for so long! Oh my gosh!"

Her momma laughed. "Go and get ready. I'm making fried chicken and veggies."

Lena hugged her momma. She knew it wasn't considered "cool" to hug your mom at seventeen, but the elation she was feeling had to be let out somehow. Besides, she loved her momma and didn't see anything wrong with it. "What should I wear!" she shrieked, bouncing up the stairs without waiting for an answer. It had to be perfect. After all, she'd loved Danny since first grade, though he had been in fifth.!

He was their neighbor two houses down, and his momma was her momma's best friend. Unfortunately, that had always been a hindrance more than something that might help. At first she was excited that he would be over so often, but then he began treating her like a little sister, and then like a friend. That, she knew, was the kiss of death. Now he was twenty-one, and in college, and he was visiting her!

Twenty minutes later she was freshly showered and perfumed. She'd decided to plait her hair into a single braid down her back, and had opted for the orange sundress that flowed all the way down to her feet. Danny had always liked long dresses. She remembered him telling her once that he preferred a girl in a long dress to anything trashy. Secretly she had been glad. It meant she had a chance. She slid on her flip-flops and started to bound down the stairs, stopping when she heard muffled voices coming from the living room. Her momma called it the parlor.

Sliding her flippies off, she made her way down the dark wooden stairs, making sure to avoid the sixth stair from the top, as it had the loudest squeak she'd ever heard. Situating herself on the third stair from the bottom, she listened.

"What do you intent to do, Mona?" her momma was asking.

"I don't know."

"Surely you've told Mark it's not his."

"How can I?" Mona sniffled. "He's wanted a baby for so long and we've tried. God, Loni, we have tried so hard to have a baby and never have. I thought there was something wrong with me, but that was obviously inaccurate…"

There was a pause and Lena thought for sure that she'd been spotted, but she heard her mother shift on the sofa and she guessed that she had just moved to be beside her sister.

"What am I going to do, Loni?" Mona sobbed.

"What do you want to do?"

"I don't know."

Lena heard her momma suck air between her two front teeth. She always did that when she was at a loss for words.

"You've got to think about that first, honey," her momma said. "And then the rest will come."

"I just wish I'd never met him."

"I know," her momma soothed. "I know."

Lena started to peek around the corner, stopping when she heard a tapping on the screen door. She looked up to see Danny standing there, a group of daisies in his hand.

"Hey," he said.

She jumped up, glancing guiltily into the parlor as she passed by. "Danny!" she exclaimed, partly because she was so nervous, but also to let her momma and Aunt know they now had company. "You're early!"

"I'm sorry," he said. "I just couldn't wait."

"Momma told me you came by earlier," she said, holding the door open for him. He entered, and she took the flowers from him. "Thank you," she said, breathing them in. "They're lovely."

"No problem." He was looking in the parlor.

Lena looked back at the look of horror on her Aunt's face. She was embarrassed because Danny had been invited in during such a vulnerable time. Lena smiled her apology, the slight kind of smile her momma always gave when she was sorry for something that wasn't really her fault. "Come on, Danny, let's go put these in some water."

He couldn't tear his eyes away from the parlor as she pulled him down the hall and into the kitchen. "What's wrong with your Aunt?"

"I dunno," she said, opening up her mother's hutch to grab a crystal vase. It was her favorite. "Some kind of problems with my Uncle, I think."

"Really?"

"Yeah." She took a seat at her momma's old country table situated just to the left of the cooking area. She patted the padded seat next to her and Danny took his place. "So, what did you want earlier?" she asked. "Momma told me you stopped by to see me."

"Huh? Oh, I just thought I should come by and say hi while I was here. I am headed back to school and won't be back for a few months."

"Well that was sweet of you." She smiled, trying to bat her eyes like other girls she'd seen. She crossed her legs, making sure to demonstrate for him how long her skirt was.

"Nice dress," he said.

"Thank you." She couldn't stop smiling.

"Lena!" her momma called from the parlor. "Come here please!"

Lena looked at Danny and shrugged her shoulders. "I'll be right back."

Her momma was standing at the foot of the stairs when she made it to the foyer, worry creasing her brow.

"What's wrong?" Lena asked.

"Honey, I need you to go upstairs and find that yellow quilt your great Grammy made."

"But we don't know what trunk it's in. Why do you need a quilt anyway? It's pretty warm in here."

"I don't. Your Aunt Mona needs it. It's her favorite one. Please, honey, just do it."

Lena nodded, looking back for only a moment toward the kitchen, and made her way up the stairs.

She would probably remember that afternoon for her whole life. At least that is what she assumed. Because as she was searching through the quilt trunk at the end of her momma's bed she heard the screen door to the back open, that familiar creak disrupting the lazy afternoon, and then snap shut with a loud thud.

First she heard her Aunt Mona's sobs, and then a soothing "shhh…"

Having located the requested quilt in the very bottom of her mother's chest, she held it to her abdomen and made her way over to the window. Situating herself on the window ledge, she looked down into the garden and to the scene unfolding. Yes, her Aunt Mona was there, and she was still sobbing. She felt sorry for her.

"Mona, stop crying," she heard a male voice say, but it wasn't her daddy and it wasn't her Uncle. She squinted her eyes against the sun.

"Danny," she exclaimed, though the parties below didn't hear her.

He squatted on the ground before her, taking her hands into his. "Everything is going to be okay," he said.

Lena thought it was sweet that he was trying to make this older woman feel better. He was definitely the kind of guy she could see herself growing old with. Not that she was planning her golden years just yet. She settled against the window frame, her young heart swooning.

"How can you say that!" Mona exclaimed. "I am pregnant."

"I know."

Lena rose up, leaning out a little farther.

"You know, yet you can tell me everything is going to be okay?" She stood up. "What am I supposed to tell my husband?"

"Tell him that you fell in love with someone that treats you right." He followed her frantic paces around the yard. Finally he grabbed her, turning her to him. "Someone who can give you what you need."

She laughed. "You're a child. You're in college."

"I'm in love with you!" Danny exclaimed, holding her hands tight, though she was trying to break free.

Lena fell back, her head knocking hard against the frame of the window.

"How can you love me?" she heard her Aunt Mona ask. "I'm too old for you. You should be with someone like Lena. She's young and lovely and…"

"A *child*," he finished. "I want you."

Lena stood up. Her head ringing from both the knock against the frame and the sting of the words uttered by the only boy she'd ever loved.

"Lena, honey, what's wrong?" her momma asked as she stepped down from the last stair. "Lena," her momma shook her, pulling her head around. "You're crying. Honey, what's wrong?"

She didn't speak, but there must have been something in her eyes because her mother smiled. It was that slight kind of smile she gave when she was apologizing for something that wasn't her fault. Her momma pulled her into a warm embrace and Lena allowed it.

"You were right, momma," she sobbed. "Curiosity does kill." It had certainly killed something in her.

Ladyfingers

Savannah Morton hadn't been home in years. Three years to be exact. She'd been too busy trying to get her business off the ground to even think of returning. Now, as she looked at the large craftsman home that had been in her family for more than half a century, she questioned why it had all been more important than coming back home for a couple of days now and then.

She surveyed the wide gallery, still adorned with a swing for two and wide-bottom rockers. The Mortons were a small-bottomed family, but they loved having room to move. At least that's what her Grams had always said. Many summers had been spent in those rockers stringing beans or husking corn when the back porch didn't suit them. She'd hated it then. Well, in a way. The forest green color of the house contrasted well with the sienna trim, and the standard lace curtains still served to obscure the view of passersby, while still affording a good deal of light to the formal dining and living rooms.

Her feet moved tentatively toward the cement stairs, her mind wandering back to summer nights spent with Jacob McKinney and Star Thurston, just a group of pre-teens staring at the stars and making big plans for the future. None of which included remaining in their hodunk little town. The kitten heel of her sandal sent a 'clud' shuddering across the porch, taking her back to winter days spent clearing snow and spring games of hide and seek. She sat on the swing, closing her eyes against the soft breeze that greeted her movement.

She'd just begun to drift back when another 'clud' on the porch forced her back into the present. Standing there in a paisley colored polo and relaxed fit jeans was the boy she'd never expected to see again.

"Vanna?" he said, his tone a question.

She wondered if she had really changed that much. It had only been five years since they'd seen one another. "Actually," she said standing, "I go by Savannah now."

He smiled, his full lips pulling back to expose ultra-white teeth. He was still cute, she thought as he began to fumble in the large manila envelope he held for something. Once his treasure, a set of keys, had been found he pushed his fingers through the raven-colored mop on his head and laughed. "I thought I'd lost them."

He dangled the key ring and its companions from his forefinger. The keychain with her company's name on it hanging lowest. Her heart lurched seeing it there. It had been delivered by parcel, not hand. It was a shame she would never live down.

"Shall we go in?" he asked. "I mean, are you ready to go in?"

She nodded.

He turned the key, pushing open the maple door whose six windows had always seemed too high for her. Even now she would have to stand on the very tips of her toes to get a good look outside. They stepped into the foyer and he placed the keys on the small table by the door. The movement struck her and she had to swallow the lump burning the back of her throat. It was just as her grandmother had always done.

"There's a family," he was saying. "That is interested if you're looking to sell."

She looked at him, hating him just a little for suggesting it. "What makes you think I want to sell?"

"I guess we just figured because you haven't been home... I mean, you just seem pretty happy in Charlotte."

She stepped into the formal living room, turning on him as the last words escaped his mouth. "And how would you, or anyone else in this town, know that? She quipped.

He was sorry he'd presumed, she could tell by the way he averted his gaze from her, and the step back he'd taken at her response. If she hadn't been so damned angry she might have felt bad.

The living room was as it had always been. The fireplace was center of the side wall, just to the right of the large picture window. In the corner was an old Magnavox radio perched atop a telephone table, and in the other corner her own mother's curio cabinet full of figurines she'd been fond of collecting. Savannah's hand fell on the old leather chair before her. "Everything is the same," she whispered. The same as it had been three years ago when she'd packed up everything and gone. She'd left it all behind over a broken heart. She'd left her behind.

"We haven't touched anything," he said from his place by the stairs.

"I can tell." She wiped the rogue tear winding its way over her cheek. "This was my grandfather's chair. He used to spend hours in here after supper reading the evening paper and listening to the radio. Grams was going to get rid of it about five years ago. All of it, even the Magnavox, but..." She stopped, trying desperately to maintain her composure.

He nodded, never moving from his place by the stairs.

She turned, walking past him and into the formal dining room. As in the living room, nothing had changed. She continued into the kitchen, the one room she'd managed to get her grams to update. She ran a shaking hand along the granite counter top installed four years before. That had been a remodel to remember. She'd known what she wanted, but then again she always did. The open-faced cabinets still held her favorite dishes, and in the sink- bottom up- was the coffee mug she'd purchased for her at a book fair when she was twelve. The words were faded now, but the faint outline of #1 Grandma was still visible. She picked it up, turning it over in her hands. It was possibly the last thing her grams had touched. She'd given it to her for mother's day.

"You okay?" he asked behind her.

She nodded. "Yes, Jacob, I'm fine."

"Hey," he said in a *look at you* kind of way.

She turned to look at him. "What?"

"I thought you'd forgotten my name."

She managed a chuckle. "Not in the slightest."

He smiled and she was grateful for it. Their meeting could have been much more awkward. In fact, he took a great chance coming out to meet her. She tried to think of what her Grams might have done to him, had she known he was the reason for her leaving.

She held up the cup. "Do you remember when I bought this mug?"

"Seventh grade," he said.

She laughed. "Only grams would use the same coffee mug for twenty years." She placed it back into the drop sink, bottom up. "Excuse me for a moment, please," she said, making her way toward the back door.

Her hand fell on the knob, but she didn't turn it right away. She was bracing herself for what was on the other side. One part of her hoped it would be in ruin, that her Grams would have allowed their oasis to become overgrown, but when she opened the door she found it was all the same.

On the back porch were their two chairs, and on either side a metal bowl for collecting their spoils. She sat in the chair that had always been her grandmother's, running her hands along the smooth armrests. She imagined for a moment that her Grams was there, but the moment passed and she stood, grabbing the watering can and heading out to the small garden they'd kept every year since she was seven.

As she weeded around the blossoms and sprouts of the most recently planted crops she began to sob. "I'm so sorry, Grams," she said. "I should have been here." She dropped the watering can, burying her face in her hands. "I'm so sorry," she cried.

"Well, lookie here," she heard a familiar voice say. "Do you know what those are, little Anna?"

She stopped sobbing, her head snapping up. "Grams?" She searched for any sign of the only mother she had ever really known, but she was completely alone. Not even Jacob had ventured out. She pulled her knees to her chest, resting her forehead on the bony knobs. Rocking back and forth she wished harder than she had ever wished before for her Grams to be with her. "I'm so sorry I wasn't here," she said, tears returning. "I love you."

"Look at these ladyfingers," she heard her Grams say.

"Why do they call them ladyfingers?" Savannah asked, hanging on to the moment by keeping her eyes closed tight.

"You know, I don't rightly know, but they sure do taste good."

Her chuckle rode away on the breeze.

Savannah opened her eyes, moving over to the place where they'd always planted the ladyfingers. She popped off the ones that were ready. Jacob joined her, his red-rimmed eyes soft and concerned.

"We used to tend this garden together," she said. "She taught me everything I know." She looked up at him. "I loved her so much."

"She loved you too," he said, but she could tell he knew he hadn't needed to.

She nodded. "I know." She stood up, dusting off the black dress she'd been wearing for three days. Had she been gone three days? "I guess I'll be taking care of it on my own from now on," she said with a sniffle.

"You're moving back?" he asked, his blue eyes bright.

"Yeah, I think I am. I should have never gone."

"What about your business?"

She rolled the ladyfingers around in her hands. "I guess this town could use a sweet shoppe better than Charlotte." She held up her hands. "Now, she said, "How do you feel about okra?"

Reunion

There comes a time in everyone's life that they must own up to something they've done. Some call it karma, and some call it come-uppins. Call it what you will. Sarah Jane figured that she might just call it inevitable.

She had never been proud of the person she'd been in school. Even as a teen every time she would shove Janice Sneeker into the locker on passing, she hated herself a little more. It had been even worse after she'd received the distinct honor of prom queen. What she didn't get to accomplish in high school she moved on to do in college. Mind you, there wasn't as much time for nonsense and queen bee-ness in college, she still managed to get it in and maintain her 3.5 GPA.

She imagined now that she had felt some sense of entitlement. Her parents had always told her she was a special child. Her father gave in easily to her whims, working extra hours just to be able to buy her that BMW she wanted as her first car as opposed to the Honda they'd found in their price range. Her mother didn't give in so easily, which caused more tension than she cared for at home, but as long as she'd been given her way everything worked out for the best. For everyone.

But now was the time for owning up. She stepped out of the BMW she'd been driving for fifteen years, straightening the Kathy Ireland jumpsuit she'd managed to save enough money to purchase for the occasion, and made her way through the double doors to face up to those she'd been so horrible to so long ago.

It's hard to describe what she thought as she made her way to event room B. Even harder to describe what she was feeling.

The question her mind pondered was, why did we even show up? No one in high school cared what has happened to us. Not even Amber, the best friend Sarah Jane thought she'd ever have, gave one fig about what had happened to her, where she'd disappeared to, or why she had never managed to graduate college.

She'd heard the talk around town. Poor little spoiled girl. Maybe if she hadn't been so damned hateful her life might have turned out better. Nothing had hurt worse, though, than when she'd heard Amber telling Davis, Sarah Jane's high school sweetheart, about her select loser status.

How could one fall so far?

Olivia Jacobs was seated at an expansive table before a set of double doors that Sarah Jane assumed would lead into the party. She looked radiant. She was no longer sporting the multi-colored pigtails from senior year (that was a great senior pic). Instead her hair was wrapped in a loose bun on top of her head, with light brown tendrils framing her oval face and falling to the bulge under the 70s inspired gown frock she wore.

"Sarah Jane!" she squealed. "You look great!"

The first lie of the night, Sarah Jane thought to herself. "Thank you," she said smiling, as Olivia pulled her in for a hug over the surface of the table.

Sarah Jane held her back, worried she might injure the baby nestled in her womb. Olivia pulled her ruby lips back in a smile.

"What do you think" she asked, turning to show her profile. "Hard to believe, huh?"

"Y-yes," Sarah Jane answered. "When are you due?"

"Got a few more months to go." She rubbed the bulge and then grabbed a large square sticker from the table. "Here's your name tag. Not that you need it!"

Sarah Jane smiled, though the stab was received successfully. She only hoped this night wouldn't end for her like it had for Carrie White in the famous novel. "Thanks," she said.

She stepped away from the table, peeling the shiny back off of the large blue square with "Hello, my name is Sarah Jane Thatcher" written smack dab in the center.

She looked back at the door that would lead her away from this madness. The door that would keep her from facing up to the terrible things she had done. How could anyone ever atone for unnecessary cruelty?

"Sarah Jane, is that you?"

She turned to meet the eyes of Harper Noone, the one boy she'd been madly in love with from middle school until the night he announced his upcoming marriage to Amber. He had never known. "Harper, h-hi," she managed.

"You going in?"

She shook her head. "I thought about it, but I don't think so." She tried to back away, but his arm was around her shoulders, pulling her along with him toward the double doors that would, most certainly, lead to her undoing. "Harper, I don't want to go in there," she said, pulling away from him. She was to Event Room A before he caught up with her.

"Hey," he said, grabbing her arm. "What's up? I've never known you to shy away from a party."

She wanted to correct him. She wanted to tell him that she hadn't been to a proper party in ten years, but instead she just said, "I just don't feel like going in there."

He looked confused. "Why? It's our fifteen year reunion. Don't you want to go inside and see what everyone has become?"

"No, I really don't." She longed to be honest, to just confess and scream to him, *I'd love to see what they've become, but I don't want them to see what I've become!* Instead she just kept shaking her head. "I realized that I have a big meeting in the morning."

"Really?"

She shook her head. "Yeah. I've got to…" What could she say? Everyone in town knew she didn't have that kind of a job. What kind of meeting could a grocery store checker have? Aside from the super-lame quarterly meeting her boss was so fond of. She slouched against the wall. "I just can't."

His face softened and she got a glimpse of the boy she'd loved a long time ago. Not that he was bad looking now. Fifteen years had been good to him. His baby face was gone, replaced with the scruffy look of a hard-working man. He owned his own company. She knew that because of Amber, of course. He'd begun the business as soon as he'd graduated college, while Amber went on to get her master's degree and then her doctorate. Sarah Jane had wanted that life.

"Don't worry," he said, pulling her back up. "I'll stick with you."

She smiled through her mask of self-loathing. "Thanks. But what about Amber?"

"What about her? She might be inside somewhere." He started leading her back toward the double doors of doom and she allowed him to, deciding it was best to just give up and go with the flow. She seemed to play that part really well. "Though I don't know why you would want to see her. She's never been that great of a friend to you."

Sarah Jane laughed. "Way to sell out your wife."

He pushed open the double doors and she went rigid with fear. If it hadn't been for the strong arm now around her waist she might have stayed frozen there.

All eyes seemed to avert to them. Harper greeted them all with a wave and a smile. She offered her own pitiful smile, though she knew they could all see through to her cowardly little core.

"What's up, Harper!" Kyle Dupre said, giving his best friend of a decade and a half ago a high five. "Hey, Sarah Jane!" he said, giving her a wink.

"Hey, Kyle," she managed.

They were fully inside the room now. A room full of mid-thirties stood around in their Sunday bests. Some wore power suits, while some took a more relaxed and casual approach. Along the wall were photos from their senior yearbook. She found her own photo in the center of the right wall.

Had her eyes really been that bright? She stopped, staring at the girl from her past, wondering just where she'd gone.

"I'll be right back," Harper said, leaning in so that she might hear over the music of ages past. "I'm going to get us some drinks."

She nodded, her eyes never moving from that giant black and white photo of her and Davis just after they'd won prom queen and king.

"It's hard to believe I was ever that cute, huh?" Someone said, their stale breath wafting across the small divide.

She turned to face the boy she'd given her virginity to, startled by how handsome he still looked. It was as if time had somehow reversed and they were as they had been, him drunk and amorous and her full of self-hatred. Maybe that's why she had been so nasty to everyone.

Maybe not.

"Still touting on about how great you are, I see," she said feigning a smile.

"I just thought it might be a good way to open a conversation," he said with a shrug.

"I'm shocked you could be so clever after having a few drinks. You've definitely changed."

He laughed, pulling her into a crushing embrace. "How have you been?" he asked, releasing her.

She shrugged. "Fine, I guess. How about you?" She looked back at the photo. "Still king?"

"Left that behind a long time ago. I'm an architect now. "

She smiled. His one big dream in high school had been to be just that. They used to lie under the large oak outside the library and talk about what they wanted to do. She had big dreams of being a journalist, while he wanted to be a big-time architect. He wanted to design the next great thing.

"That's fantastic!" It was the most genuine that she'd felt all night. "What big city did you decide to settle in? New York? Los Angeles?"

"Houston."

"Really?"

He chuckled. "Yeah. It's not as romanticized as New York or LA, but I like it." He pushed a stray brown lock from his forehead, the gold on his left hand catching the light as he did.

"Oh my gosh," she squealed. "You're married!"

He looked at the ring as if he'd forgotten. "Yes, ma'am."

"How long? Is she here? Where is she? What's her name? What's she like?"

"Six years," he said with a chuckle. "She's back in Houston. She couldn't get the week off from work."

"What does she do?"

Harper returned, handing her a hurricane goblet with an orange and pink umbrella sticking out of a line of fruit. She smiled her thanks as she accepted it and he nestled in to her left.

"She's a feature writer for a Latin magazine out there. "

"You married a Latina," she said with a smile. "Very nice. I wish I could have met her."

"Maybe at the twentieth."

She nodded. "I'll look forward to it."

David looked around, nodding to someone across the room. "I gotta go. Bruce promised me he'd beat me at pool. I didn't have the heart to tell him that he's gonna lose." He kissed her cheek, giving her shoulders a squeeze. "Take care, JayJay."

Why he even dubbed her JayJay she would never know. The one time she'd asked him he'd only shrugged. He asked if she wanted him to stop calling her that, but she had kind of liked it. No one had a nickname for her now days.

No good ones anyway.

She turned to Harper. "I can't believe Davis is married!" she shrieked. "I thought he would be a playboy until his fifties."

He laughed, then leaned over and said the name she'd been dreading since walking through that first set of double doors. "I just saw Janice Sneeker over by the bar. She was asking about you."

She looked around like a madwoman suffering from paranoid delusions. "Where is she? Did she see me?"

"Yeah. I told her you were here by your photo talking to Dave. She said she's coming over."

She looked at him. A part of her wanted to backhand him, to scream at him until he cried. How could he? Did he not remember how horrible she had been to that girl? How could she ever face her? But the other part of her was ready to taste the bitter pill of revenge.

She looked fabulous, just as Sarah Jane had expected. In high school she'd been a tiny girl; just over five and a half feet, with knobby knees and stringy red hair. She'd been the butt of all jokes, and Sarah Jane felt that hers had probably been the most frequent. The woman that approached them now was on the other side of that spectrum. Tall and lovely, with closely cropped red hair and the deep complexion of someone who'd spent the last two weeks on an island in the Caribbean, this version of Janice made Sarah Jane feel inadequate.

Not that she needed the help.

"Sarah Jane," Janice said, her voice like honey. "Look at you!" She pulled Sarah Jane into an embrace, then held her out at arm's length. "You haven't changed a bit."

She was right.

"H-hi, Janice."

"No one calls me Janice anymore. I go by my middle name." She pointed to the tag on her fuller bosom.

Implants? She wouldn't dare ask Janice or anyone else.

"Call me Abigail," she said with a toothy smile.

Veneers. Had to be.

Why couldn't she stop! For ten years she'd done nothing but loathe herself for having picked on Janice, and now she couldn't stop pointing out the little "improvements" the girl had made along the way.

"You look great, Jan... I mean, Abigail."

"So do you!" she fawned. She looked at Harper, her eyes gobbling him up. "So do you, Harper," she added with a wink.

Sarah Jane looked back at him. She wondered if she should wipe the drool from the corner of his mouth for him.

Why was she jealous?

Amber, she reminded herself. He's married to Amber.

"What have you been up to?" She asked Abigail.

"I'm a writer," she gushed.

It was like a punch in the gut. "R-really?" Sarah Jane took a gulp of the fruity cocktail Harper had supplied her.

"Yes."

"What have you had published?"

"Jersey's Way. Have you heard of it?"

Ten weeks at number one, Sarah Jane thought, who hadn't heard of it? She smiled. "That is fantastic."

While she'd meant it with Davis she just couldn't manage sincerity with her nemesis. The years of guilt were beginning to subside and she could feel the old Sarah Jane waking from her slumber.

"I know. I still can't really believe it." She laughed, throwing her head back to expose her long graceful neck.

"I didn't know you wanted to be a writer," Harper chimed in. "Didn't you want to be a teacher?"

She smiled at him, her eyes narrowing in a *come hither* kind of way. Sarah Jane knew it all too well. She'd had that same look once. "I can't believe you even knew that!" she said, giving him a flirty shove. "I *am* a teacher!"

Harper nodded and Abigail smiled. She knew that he was falling into her trap. Sarah Jane took a step away from the two of them.

"Really?" he asked.

"Uh-huh," she said, wrapping her ruby lips around the pink silly straw sticking up out of her glass.

It was disgusting.

"I taught English until the book was published. Had to take time off to travel and promote." She gave Sarah Jane a wink

"Will you go back?" he asked.

She had him and she knew it. Sarah Jane stepped back, leaning against the cool speckled paper of the wall, watching the new master. She wondered when Abigail came to be. Had it happened when Janice went off to college and discovered a life beyond the strict confines of her mother and father's home? Or had it been after enduring years of abuse from the kids she'd grown up with? Had she decided that she would become a vixen in college, or afterward to thwart any acts of cruelty?

Sarah Jane surveyed the room, looking from one face to another. She'd known them all in one way or another. Some had been in her circle of friends, while others had been the target for her unhappiness, or the unhappiness of her counterparts. The only one that had never really fit in had been Harper. If it hadn't been for Amber he wouldn't have come near their group. He'd made it known more than once that they were all monsters in his opinion.

Was it really any wonder that Abigail had him eating out of the palm of her hand?

But it was. Wasn't it?

Sarah Jane realized her limitations. She hated her life, hated the circumstances that she'd been thrust into. She was the laughingstock of her entire town. A loser. In effect, she had become Janice. And Janice had become Abigail, a tanner more enhanced version of Sarah Jane.

Her stomach turned. Placing the now-empty goblet down on the nearest table she made her way through the double doors, down the hall, and out into the balmy June evening.

By the time she reached her two-door, baby blue beamer her make up ran in rivers down her face. She had been a fool to come. You can't recapture that which you've lost. Or something like that.

She pulled open the door, tossing her clutch into the passenger seat.

"Where are you off to?" Harper asked making it to the car just before she collapsed inside.

She dabbed her eyes with the embroidered handkerchief that had once belonged to her grandmother. "I shouldn't have come," she sniffled. "I should have known better."

"Why shouldn't you be here? Didn't you go to high school with us?"

"I'm a horrible person."

"Sarah Jane, you're being too hard on yourself."

She jerked her head up, allowing him to see the pathetic human being she'd become. "Really? I don't think I'm hard enough on myself." She slammed the car door closed, making her way across the parking lot to the man-made pond created especially for special occasions.

Harper followed her, leaning up against one of the tall oak trees that lined the pond. She remembered when they'd planted them. In fact, if she remembered correctly, she and her mother had planted the very tree he was leaning against.

"What happened to you, Sarah Jane?" he asked, his voice soft enough to break her heart.

The one boy she had ever loved, who never seemed to notice she was alive, wanted to know what happened to her.

"Life happened," she spat. "While the rest of you were off getting college degrees and building your lives I was here, rotting to death in this town, wishing I was anywhere else." She dropped down on the grass, kicking the ten dollar pumps she'd purchased after work off her feet. "Now Janice Skeener has taken over my life." She laughed, a sad sort of eruption lacking any emotion. "Who would have thought…"

"You really wanted to be like that?"

She looked at him. "You seemed to like it."

"That's the way things like that are," he said. "You see it from afar looking all shiny and perfect. You get this idea that it's just that. And then you get closer and notice the little imperfections. Not that imperfections aren't lovely in their own right. I happen to love imperfections."

"Then you've just discounted your entire point."

"No, I haven't. What I mean to say is, you are fooled by the flash of a smile or the curve of a hip. It isn't until you get up close that you see the cracks in the veneer to what is really beneath."

She nodded. "I think I see your point."

"So, what have you been doing with yourself?" he asked, turning to face her.

"Well, when I was entering my junior year my dad and mom were in a car accident. Dad died after a few days in the hospital, but mom made it. She was a forty-five year old, highly educated woman reduced to the functions of a seven year old. I left school to take care of her. Got myself a fine job at the local supermarket where I am senior cashier. That's right. I am awesome." She dared a look at him, but his eyes had transfixed on the horizon. She shrugged and continued, "Six months ago my mom died of a stroke. I would just kill myself, but I'm afraid the punishment would just get worse."

"Punishment?"

"Oh yeah. I was a nasty bitch to everyone. My mom and dad were taken away because they were the only ones that could love me the way I was. My future was taken away and given to the person I was the worst to. And now I am bound to marry some loser and have ten kids I can't support only to be cheated on and left to raise the heathens on my own."

He chuckled.

"Is this funny to you?" She quipped.

"That last part is a little dramatic, don't you think?"

"No."

"Your parents didn't get taken away from you because you were a mean girl," he said after a few tense moments. "I don't think karma would be so cruel."

"You have no idea how horrible I was."

"I was married to your best friend. I think have an idea."

She shrugged. "I guess."

"And Janice worked hard for what she has, so I highly doubt that she would agree with the hypothesis that it was taken from you and *given* to her."

"Maybe."

"Being a cashier is a noble profession."

"If you say so," she snorted.

"My mother was a cashier until I made her my bookkeeper."

She lowered her head. "I'm sorry."

He was silent for a moment longer and then turned to her. "You can't keep allowing your regrets to rule your life, Sarah Jane. You're not a loser, and your life is most certainly not over. All you have to do is let go of your fear and the anger at your circumstances. So you didn't get to your dreams when the rest of us did. So what? You've got plenty of time to make them happen."

He looked back out at the water, then said, "I need to know one thing."

"What?" she asked, still wallowing in the pit of self-pity.

"Are you engaged?"

She laughed. "No."

"No prospects at all?"

"Not for me. I guess I should have added that to my list."

He moved closer. "You haven't asked me what I have been up to."

"Because I already know. You married Amber out of high school. You started your own company out of college and she is some big shot college professor. You don't have any children. You're blissfully…"

"Divorced."

She looked at him. "What?"

"Amber and I are divorced."

"When?"

"A few years ago."

"Why?"

"She found that she liked teaching a little too much. She kept working late, if you know what I mean."

"Oh my goodness, Harper, really?"

"Oh yeah. So we got a divorce. She is living in South Dakota with her lover."

"I'm so sorry."

"Don't be."

"Then it will be okay for you to go home with Abigail," she jabbed.

"Not interested." He leaned closer and she found her hand going to the brown bun situated at the back of her head.

It was a tick she had developed when she became self-conscious. She'd tried for years to break it with no success. "Why not?" she dared to ask.

"Because there is this girl I've had my eye on for a long time."

"Who's that?" she asked, her tone a little more playful this time, leaning in to meet him. She held her breath awaiting his answer. The Sarah Jane she'd thought long-dead awakened from her slumber, posed to pounce at the slightest hint that it was she he wanted.

"This girl I've known for a long time. She's got a lot of hang ups, but I think she's really cute."

She smiled. "Anyone I know?"

Blossom

I try not to be too much like my family. They're mountain folk, you see, and they tend to get all fired up over nothing, especially when it comes to a person they decide not to like. Half the time it's because they're already predisposed to not liking them, but the other half of the time it is cause of something the fiend has said, or been rumored to have said. I've tried to keep the peace and tell them there's no use always getting so mad, but they tell me I am too "educated" and that I just don't understand the ways of my own people.

Who are they to tell me I don't understand? I live with them. I see them. I just don't understand why they waste so much energy getting so mad over nothing.

"One of these days you're gonna understand, Alma Mae." That's what they tell me.

But how can I understand something that is so perplexing?

"Alma Mae, it's time to go," Kitt, my little sister said, poking her nosey little head through the crack in my door.

I'm not allowed to close it. Not all the way. Momma says that closed doors are for when you've got something to hide. I have tried to tell her a million times that's not always the case, but she just shakes her head and waves me off.

"Kitt!" I shrieked, trying to grab at my journal. She was always trying to read my writing. Not that she was much good at it. She was only in first grade. She released it pretty quickly when I jerked the door open and hovered over her. "You know better," I chided. "This is my personal journal. My eyes only. See," I pointed to the front of the composition book where I'd written *MY EYES ONLY!*

"You're always writin' in that stupid book. Momma says you'd rather write in there than talk to us!"

"Maybe I would," I snipped.

She crossed her tiny arms over her narrow waist, looking just like Momma, and stuck her bottom lip out. I could never stay mad when she did this, which, I suspect, is why she was always doing it.

"Hey," I said, ruffling her chin length brown curls. "You know I didn't mean that, Kitt. I'm sorry." Tucking my journal under one arm, I wrapped the other one around her shoulders, squeezing slightly. "How could I not like talkin' to you?"

She smiled and I was grateful. With my conflicting views I didn't have many friends within my family. Besides, Kitt is my only baby sister. I couldn't go around alienating her all the time. Even though, at fifteen I did it quite often.

"So, where are we goin'?" I asked as we walked through the small farmhouse we'd both inhabited since birth toward the front door where Momma was waiting. Daddy never waited. He was always the first one in the car. Dealing with getting the kids ready was woman's work. At least that's how he'd always been taught. Sadly, Momma has never made him think any differently.

"Gotta go to Aunt Jane's."

I groaned. Not because I don't like Aunt Jane, mind you. In fact, she was my favorite Aunt. She's the youngest of my mother's sisters. When I was younger she would let me come and hang out with her at grandmama's house and we would have the best time. She got married about seven years ago at the tender age of eighteen, and has been pretty unavailable since. My parents thought they were hiding why pretty well from me, but I know when something's not right, and my Uncle Ford is not right.

"Why do we have to go there now?" I whined.

"Momma didn't say. She just said we have to get there now, so we'd better get."

I could tell by the look on my Momma's face that something was wrong. Her gray eyes were cloudy and rimmed in red. But I didn't dare ask. If she wanted me to know she would tell me.

I think.

Aunt Jane and Uncle Ford lived about six miles from us, unless you counted the length of their driveway. That would put them six and a quarter miles from us. I guess it's customary to include that, so I will.

Their house up on the mountain afforded them a privacy that not everyone would understand. Sure they had a neighbor or two, but a heck of a lot of noise would have to be made for them to hear anything. I think that's why Aunt Jane's unhappiness went unnoticed for so long. She never came down the mountain. Not really. Maybe once or twice in a month. Momma would carry us up there once in a while just to check on her. Uncle Ford would be working out on his old Dodge Ram.

My Daddy always laughs when Momma talks about it. A Ford drivin' a Dodge was just about the funniest thing he'd ever heard, or so he always says.

Then Kitt and I are sent to our rooms and I can hear Momma talkin' to him in hushed tones. I know she's talking to him about the bruise she glimpsed on Aunt Jane's arm, or the shiner that's turned to a light green right around her pretty blue eyes.

"Come on, girls, let's hurry," Momma said, as we loaded into the Chevy truck my Daddy loved more than life itself.

I will never understand the bond between a man and his truck.

It was a quiet ride. Momma looked out the passenger window and Daddy stared straight ahead. Kitt and I exchanged glances once or twice, but we didn't dare disrupt the silence. I did the only thing I knew to do. I opened my journal and began to write, but that didn't hold my attention long. Something was terribly wrong and I could feel it all the way down.

"I want you girls to stay outside now," Momma said breaking the silence, when we pulled to a stop in front of the small frame house.

There were cars all over the yard. I recognized them as my mother's family. All three of her older sisters and her older brother, as well as a few grown cousins seemed to be there. There were men sitting on the front porch and women darting in and out of the double screen doors. I wanted more than anything to go inside. I even wanted to protest to my Momma that it was still too chilly to be sitting outside when there was a perfectly good fire going in the house. I could tell by looking at the chimney that one had been started, but my Momma was already on the porch, pulling open one of the screen doors, and my Daddy was already consorting with the men sitting outside.

"You wanna play?" Kitt asked.

"Why don't you go and find Hazel," I suggested. "I'm just gonna go up under the sugar tree and write in my journal."

"Fine."

She was pouting again.

"Hey," I said. "How often do you even see Hazel? Don't you think she would want to play with you? You know you're her favorite cousin."

"Can I come play with you later?"

I smiled. "Sure."

I made my way across the yard, once I was sure Kitt was set to play with Hazel, and settled in at the base of the tree. The views weren't much at this time of year. Early March was still brown mostly, with a patch of thick green grass here and there. It made everything look kind of like it had the mange. At least that is what I have always thought.

I longed for winter to be over. It had been bitterly cold for months, with constant snow showers and accumulation. Daddy had missed more work due to the weather this year than he had in twenty years. At least that's what he always bickered about when he heard the weatherman calling for more.

"Hey, Alma Mae, what ya doin?" my cousin, Maggie May (named after the Rod Stewart song, of course) asked, sitting on the ground across from me.

"Writing," I answered simply. I detested interruption when in thought.

"You're always doin' that, huh?"

"I have to practice if I'm gonna be worth my salt as a writer when I'm older."

"You sound like you've got it all figured out," Maggie May said, stretching like a cat in what little sun was shining down. She was wearing a light sweater and Capri pants.

I pulled my fuchsia sweater tighter. Funny how the perception of cold could make you chill.

"Not everything," I said. "Just what I want to do with my life."

Maggie shrugged. "I'm goin' to college in a year and I don't even know what I'm gonna go for."

She was two years older than me, in case you haven't done the math, and she never failed to remind me at every meeting.

"You'll figure it out," I said, turning my attentions back to my journal.

"Woody says I shouldn't even bother to get an education after high school. He says no wife of his is gonna work and leave him home with the kids." She sighed. "Sometimes I think he's right, but then I look at Aunt Jane." She turned her head toward the house, her raven locks flying about as she did so.

I looked up. "What's wrong with Aunt Jane?"

"Nuthin, I guess. She's just stuck up here on this mountain all by herself while Uncle Ford goes tom-cattin' around. I don't wanna be like that. I wanna have a career and not depend on a man."

Finally she was speaking sense.

"Maggie," I said, closing my book. "Do you know what's goin' on?"

She took delight in my ignorance. The light in her green eyes told me that. She pulled her heart-shaped lips back to expose a row of beautiful white teeth. No wonder Woody didn't want her leaving this valley. She was sure to have a hundred boys falling at her feet the moment she stepped onto a college campus. They would be doing it now if they didn't all know that Woody would beat them up.

"Your Momma and Daddy didn't tell you?" She leaned closer, pulling her right knee up to her chest. "Uncle Ford's in the hospital. He might not make it."

"What happened?"

"Somebody shot him outside of Jessie Packard's place. Please don't ask me why he was at Jessie Packard's place. Your little sister would know that."

She was right, Kitt would know. Jessie lived about a mile from us back in the holler, and she always had traffic coming out of her driveway. I'd had no idea that my Uncle Ford was one of them.

"Do they know who did it?" I asked.

"They suppose that I did," Aunt Jane said, stepping out from behind the sugar tree almost scaring the life out of both of us.

I turned around, my hand flying to my mouth to stifle my surprise.

"Aunt Jane, I didn't know you were there," Maggie said, her pretty face wearing its very own flash of surprise.

"It's okay, Mags," Aunt Jane said with a smile. "I just needed to get out of that house. I love my family, but they're talkin' crazy in there."

Maggie smiled, but I could see she was very uneasy.

Aunt Jane took a seat beside me, leaning up against the base of the old maple tree. "Your Momma is lookin' for you, Maggie."

It was the excuse Maggie needed. She was up and across the yard in a flash. Aunt Jane giggled as we watched her go.

"She took off in a hurry," I said, unable to stifle my own giggle.

"I think I make her nervous." Aunt Jane stretched, her pale legs extending from under the flower housedress she was wearing to settle on the bristly grass.

She was quiet for a moment, her eyes focused on the horizon. I watched her eyes, the way they seemed to be focusing on the farthest point that she could see, and I watched as the soft breeze picked up loose strands of brown that had fallen out of the haphazard bun atop her head. There was another bruise, this one at the back of her jaw, where the lines of the face meet the side of the head. It was a light green in the shape of a thumb, or perhaps that was my imagination.

"You're always lookin' at me so close, Al," Aunt Jane said without looking away from her focal point. "Why do you do that?"

I shrugged. "I don't know. I-I'm sorry."

"It doesn't bother me. It just makes me wonder."

"Wonder what?"

She turned her head to me and said, "What you're looking for."

I dropped my head in shame.

"So what do you see?" she asked. "When you look at me."

I looked back up at her. Her eyes were focused back on the horizon.

"I-I… I see you, I guess."

She laughed and turned to look at me again. Her cheeks were damp and I realized she'd begun to cry. "And what do I look like?"

I shrugged.

"Do I look like a monster?"

I tried to stand up, but she held me in place.

"Please tell me," she said. "Because I have stared at myself and I can't see anything."

I didn't want to tell her, though I'd written about it a million times. She was the embodiment of all my characters. She was sadness and perseverance. She was strength, but also weakness. "Aunt Jane, what's going on?" I asked, trying to change the subject.

She chuckled, wiping her eyes. "It's just like Maggie told you. Your Uncle Ford has been shot," she choked out the last six words. "Someone shot him in the back when he was leaving Jessie's house. And his family thinks it was me."

"Was it?"

She laughed and my heart lurched at the sorrow I heard. "Why would you ask me that, Al?"

"Because I know."

She looked at me, seeming slightly surprised that I would admit to such knowledge. "What do you know?" she asked, picking at the bits of twigs surrounding us.

"I know why you always have bruises."

She stood up and I followed her, leaving my journal by the base of the old tree. She was at the edge of the yard, her eyes transfixed on that same spot once more. I wondered what she found there.

"I was eighteen when we got married. Stupid and full of romantic thoughts," she began explaining, though I was unsure why. "And it *was* romantic for the first little bit. He was always eager to come home to me." She dipped her head, but I saw the color rise to her cheeks. "But then he changed. He got mean sometimes. If I asked him about money or what he was doin' with his nights when he didn't come home he would give me a smack."

"Why didn't you tell someone?"

"What could they do?" She swiped at the fresh drops coming from her eyes. "At first I thought it was my fault and then I knew it was somethin' wrong in him."

"Did you tell someone? Momma? His family?"

"No," she said emphatically. "This was my choice. I chose to be with him so I was gonna stick it out, ya know?"

I didn't.

"I have been so alone," she sobbed.

I slid my arm around her waist. "It's okay," I tried to soothe.

"Now that he's in the hospital his family is accusin' me. They're sayin' the worst things around town. Now my family is all in a tissy. You know how they get."

As she rambled on I couldn't help wondering why she was pouring her heart out to a child. Especially when she had a house filled with adults ready and willing to listen and take her side.

Then I thought that might be why. It didn't matter what she said, they would all agree with her and hate him. They would hate his family and talk about how they were gonna make them pay. That's how our family did it. They couldn't stand one another most of the time, but let someone else talk against us, or be rumored to have done so. Then it was on.

"All I keep thinkin' is how much I wanted this," she sobbed. "How much I wanted to be with Ford. How much I loved him. Now I'm just so tired. I keep lookin' for some hope. Something to signal that everything is gonna be okay. And don't tell me to pray, dammit," she said, pointing her finger at me. "I've had enough of that. Nobody seems to be listenin'."

I shook my head, my silent promise to her that I wouldn't.

"I just wanna know that I'm gonna be okay again. That I won't be so damned empty."

I dropped my head, focusing on the ground below. I wished that I could comfort her in some way, to take away the pain that had been holding her back for so long, but there was nothing I could do for her. What did I think I could do? I was only fifteen for crying out loud! But still I stood on that hill as she poured her twenty-five year old heart out to me, wishing I could provide something to make her feel better. To make her the happy Aunt Jane I remembered from my early childhood.

Then, as if my thoughts had been heard racing across the cosmos, I saw it. A shade of yellow peeking through the old brown leaves Uncle Ford hadn't bothered to clean up from the lawn. I stretched my leg out, brushing the brittle sheet away.

"Aunt Jane," I said, hoping more than anything that this would work. "Look."

She looked to me first, but I quickly pointed to the ground where the yellow blossom had opened up without the knowledge of the world around it.

She stooped down, touching the petals with shaking fingers.

"It's hope," I whispered.

"It sure is," she said, cupping the blossom and then bringing her nose to it. She stayed like that for what seemed like an eternity, her face so close to that bloom that I wondered if she had some sort of way to communicate with it. "You're doing it again," she said.

"What?"

She looked up, "Staring at me."

"I just want to make sure you're okay," I said, hoping she wasn't mad.

She stood up, pulling me close, her eyes transfixing on that spot in the distance. "I know that they give you a hard time for not bein' like them," she said after a long pause. "But I think you're pretty damn special, kid."

I smiled. "Thanks."

"I guess I should get back down to the house."

She released me and I stumbled. Finding my ground quickly, I watched her as she began down the hill.

Halfway down she stopped, turning back to me. I would spend years wishing she hadn't done this, wishing that she had continued down toward the house and continued to hold her secret close, but she had stopped and turned. "Hey, Al," she said, raising her hand to shield the sudden burst of sunshine.

"Yeah?"

"It *was* me that shot him, and I hope that son of a bitch never wakes up."

Denial

Veronica Bailey was accustomed to being the one left out. From childhood she had been the girl who was either too chubby to join, or just too ugly. It came as no surprise, then, that her latest boyfriend- if he could be called that- called to say he was no longer interested. It's not like they had been seeing one another for long. Her friend Jessica had only introduced them at her office Christmas party and it wasn't even Valentine's Day.

Still, she thought she had moved past the too chubby and too ugly stages of her life. It's amazing what daily visits to the gym and more diligent skin care could do for a girl.

She opened the refrigerator, not sure what she wanted to do. Would she eat the double chocolate fudge cake from Jessica's latest office party? Or would she drink the two bottles of Duplin sweet table wine that she was saving for the next girl night?

Closing the door she decided she would do neither.

Duncan hadn't been anything close to spectacular, so why would she ruin a perfectly good caloric day on him? Instead she plopped down on the comfy over-sized chair in her living room and dialed the only number she could think to dial.

"Hello?" Her voice was muffled and rough.

Veronica smiled at the vision of her friend's sleepy face as she sat up to answer the call. "Hey, did I wake you?"

There was a shuffling and she knew that Jessica was ambling out of bed and into a room where she wouldn't bother Jacob, her new boy toy. She took comfort in the fact that he wouldn't be around any longer than Jess deemed necessary.

"It's after ten, Ronni, of course you woke me up." Veronica could hear the leather sofa squeak as her friend settled in for the conversation. "What's up?"

"Duncan dumped me."

"Are you kidding me?" Jessica said, and Veronica imagined her raking a hand through her long blond hair. She always struggled pulling her fingers through the mass of waves. Not because her hair was thick, but because she refused to brush it often. Well, unless you counted the many times she raked her lean fingers through it.

"Nope. He called me about fifteen minutes ago."

"I thought things were going so well."

"Me too. I guess."

"You guess?"

"Yeah." Veronica laughed. "I guess. I don't know. You know I have never had much luck with guys. Who can figure them out?"

Jessica sighed. "I don't know." She yawned.

"Go back to bed, Jess. I'll see you tomorrow."

"Uh-huh," she said through her yawn.

Veronica ended the call, holding the receiver to her chest. This was the third guy Jessica had attempted to set her up with in the fifteen years they'd known one another. Each and every time the guy stayed around for a few days or weeks and then bailed. She should have learned after the fiasco that was Sam. He'd only agreed to go out with her to get to Jessica. Men. Who needed them?

****

"Well you do, silly!" her mom said at breakfast the following week.

Why she had agreed to meet her mother so soon after being dumped she might never know. "I'm not so sure, Mom," she said. "I mean, relationships never seem to work out for me." She took a bite of her bacon and eggs. "Maybe I am destined to be alone..."

Her mom chewed her grapefruit, holding out her fork to signal that she would be adding valuable input as soon as she'd finished. Veronica smiled.

"What you have to ask yourself, honey," she said finally. "Is," She held Veronica's blue eyes with her own. "What will make *you* happy?"

Veronica shook her head. "I don't know. I think I would be happy to never go out with another man. Ever."

Her mother laughed.

"What? They're complicated and... brutish."

A snort escaped through the hand her mother held in front of her face. "Honey child," she choked. "Relationships are not supposed to be easy!" Raising the corner of the burgundy linen napkin to her mouth she dabbed at the drool pooling at the corners of her mouth. "You just haven't found the right person yet," she said finally. "Just give yourself time."

"Maybe you're right," Veronica said, taking another bite of her bacon and eggs. "Maybe."

****

After the latest breakfast peptalk, and mid-morning shopping, Veronica made her way over to the park, thinking that the fresh air may help to bring the situation into some sort of perspective. Besides, she had promised Jess that she would meet her for lunch in half an hour.

She settled on the wrought iron bench that had seen her through many breakups, watching the usual mothers huddled together whispering while their toddlers threw sand on one another and stole toys from the smallest of the lot. She laughed in spite of herself as she watched the interactions of the little adults. People never really changed from infancy, they just learned the rules of the world better. And developed a better vocabulary.

"Veronica?"

She turned at the sound of her name to find the face of her most recent ex only inches from her own. She rolled her eyes and turned back to face the park scene before her. "Duncan, how *nice* to see you."

He laughed. "You're kidding, right?"

She moved over as he swung around to sit next to her. "It's called being polite," she snipped.

Seemingly oblivious to the fact that they were recent ex's he asked, "What're you up to?"

She looked at him, slightly confused by his presence and overtly annoyed. "Why do you care?" she snipped. Wow, one week post break up was no time for the ex to show up.

"Just because we're not seeing one another anymore doesn't mean that I don't care."

She laughed.

"What?" he asked, an uncomfortable laugh escaping.

"I do not get men!"

He looked confused.

"You're sitting here telling me that you care how I feel, but you dumped me! We are not friends, Duncan! I am your ex-girlfriend and you are my ex-boyfriend. We are never supposed to speak again!"

"Are you really that upset that I dumped you? Or are you hurt because that is what is expected."

She dropped her head back as if looking to the heavens for an answer. "*What* are you talking about!"

He turned to face her, his left leg resting on the bench beside her. "I didn't break up with you because I don't like you. I like you a lot, but I am not going to be that guy."

"Why are you talking in code? What guy?"

He smiled and she thought for a moment how nice his smile was. "The guy that falls in love with a gay girl."

She roared. *"What!"*

He was in hot pursuit of her when she jumped up and began hurrying from him. How ludicrous could this day get! First the heart to heart with her mother and now this! She threw her hands up, jerking away from him when he grabbed her.

"How do you think I felt when I realized it?" he said, trying to keep up. "I really liked you. I mean *really*. And then I realize that the only reason I am around is so that you can be nearer to her."

She stopped, whirling on him. "Duncan, you're beginning to annoy me. No, you're way past that. You're beginning to piss me off. What are you talking about? I have never had a lesbian thought in my life!"

"Who was the first person you spoke to when we broke up?"

"You mean when you *dumped* me? I called my best friend because that's what girls do!"

"You called Jessica."

"She *is* my best friend."

"And I suppose Jacob was there?"

She rolled her eyes. "Yes."

"And she left the room to talk to you."

"Yes. Wow, you really have no concept of what it is to be polite, do you?" She threw her hands up when he stared at her apparently dumbfounded. She began to walk again wanting nothing more than to get away from him and his ludicrous ideas. "I don't get your species. Now I'm gay because I called my best friend when

I got dumped." She whirled on him once more. "I guess you're right. I'm a raging lez!"

"Veronica, come on!" He reached for her arm again, but she pulled away.

"You are a jerk, Duncan. I didn't think that until right now, but you really are. Leave me alone."

She left him standing in the park and stalked toward the cafe where she'd agreed to meet Jessica. Of all the things she had been accused of, being gay had never been one. Not that it was a bad thing, mind you. It just wasn't something that she was.

Her mother would never allow it.

Jessica was sitting at their usual table, her blond hair piled in a loose bun atop her head. Her lips were ruby today and sparkled when the light hit them. She was wearing a light blue sweater and a denim skirt that fell to her ankles.

She really was beautiful.

"Hey!" she said, jumping up to greet her friend.

Veronica maneuvered through the tables to the corner and returned the warm hug her friend offered. "Hey yourself. Nice sweater."

She smiled, smoothing it over her flat tummy. "I saw it in the window and had to have it."

They took their seats and Veronica sipped on the white chocolate cappuccino Jessica had waiting for her. "So what did you and Jacob do today?"

She shrugged. "I told him I would call him." She leaned closer, her ruby lips pulling back in a devilish smile. "I don't plan to call, of course."

"Of course," Veronica laughed. She'd known he wouldn't last long. Jessica never seemed to keep a man around for long. She liked it that way, she realized. When Jess was single they spent a lot more time together shopping, going to the movies, dinners, and any other thing they could think to do together. They were the perfect couple. Without being a couple, that is. She found herself hating Duncan a little bit more. If he hadn't made his accusations that might have never popped into her head. "So how did he take it?"

"He hadn't figured it out before he left." Jessica slumped, her ruby lips sticking out slightly in a pout. "I'm kinda bored with the guys I keep meeting."

She was speaking and Veronica tried like hell to stay focused and listen, but too many thoughts were swimming through her mind. She was certainly feeling happy about Jessica dumping this latest guy. But it was only because they could hang out more now. Right?

Digging through her bag she pulled out her phone and smiled. "I'm sorry, Jess," she said, interrupting her friend's animated plans for what they should do this evening. "Will you watch my bag? I need to make a quick call."

Jessica smiled. "Sure, but hurry. I only have half an hour left and you've barely spoken."

Stepping into the alcove that housed the powder rooms for both ladies and gents Veronica pressed the phone to her ear. After three rings a familiar voice came on the line.

"Hey, mom," she began. "Don't freak out, but I think I may be gay."

Illness

Tony hadn't been prepared for this, the complete and total lack of being him. When they'd told him he was going to die, and that it wouldn't be an easy death, a part of him had actually thought, hoped, PRAYED, that they were kidding. Some little part of him thought that someone would jump out from behind that curtain and yell, "GOT YA!"

But they hadn't.

The doctor bowed his head, as if he were hearing that *he* was the one dying and not the stunned thirty year old man sitting across that large oak desk in absolute silence.

Suddenly every cheesy "live like you're dying" movie he'd ever seen flashed through his mind. He'd even heard the story of a guy who sold everything because of his diagnosis, bought a Lamborghini and traveled all over the United States until it died. He was still alive. His prognosis had been bleak three years ago as well, and it looked like even he would outlive Tony.

"I wish I had better news for you," The doctor said standing. "But I can assure you we are going to approach this from every side and try like hell to save your life."

Tony swallowed the lump in his throat, not wanting to show the doctor the despair that was beginning to settle in.

What would he tell Lisa? They'd barely been married a year and now he was going to tell her that his body was revolting and he would be leaving her alone in a few short months.

"We want to begin the treatments as quickly as possible, Tony," His doctor was saying as he led him out of the office. "So you need to get back to us soon. No need to let this fester any longer than it already has."

Tony nodded.

Before he knew it he was standing out in the harsh midday sun, his coat in his hands. It's amazing what one thinks when he's been shoved into the face of death.

Is that what happened?

No. No. Death came looking for him. He wasn't parading around in the hopes that they would have a confrontation.

Why was he thinking of death as if it were a person?

"Hey, Tony, how are you?" Willis Grant asked, stopping. "It's been ages since we've seen you down at the pub."

The pub. Why did they have to call it a pub? He imagined because the owner was Irish and it reminded him of home. Who knows.

"Hey, Will," he stammered. "I'm still in newlywed mode. No time for pubs, man."

Willis laughed. "Those were good times. Hold onto them."

Tony pressed a hand to his chest to squelch the pain hammering into his heart. He nodded. "Yeah." throwing his coat on he added, "It was great to see you, Will, but I gotta go. Maybe I'll see you around."

"Sure, man. See ya."

Tony walked, though he felt more like he was stumbling, down the sidewalk and to his S10 pickup truck. Lisa had purchased it for him on their six month anniversary.

He hadn't married her for her money, though no one believed it. Everyone seemed to take major issue with the fact that she was ten years his senior.

"*When you're fifty she'll be sixty!*" they would say, their eyes wide and disturbed.

He had always asserted that age was nothing but a number. Now he found himself more than a little jealous that she was seeing her forties and he never would.

Once his truck was on the outskirts of town he pulled over to the shoulder and rested his forehead on the steering wheel. How was he going to tell her that their time is over before it has even begun? And how was he going to tell his family that their time with him was drawing to a close. Not that they saw much of him now days.

He tried to remember the last time he'd gone to visit his mother and father. Maybe once since the wedding. However, that was their fault. If they could just show a little tolerance where Lisa was concerned they could see him all the time, but he couldn't abide anyone speaking ill about his wife. Even his own mother.

Ill. He was ill.

How could he have used such a word?

He clutched his chest again.

Would he have a heart attack before the illness was allowed to run its course? From the description the doctor had given that might be best.

Breathing slowly he felt the pain lighten.

Panic attacks. That's what they have to be. Death would be foolish to take him before delighting in the sight of him fading away.

Death is not a person, he reminded himself. Death is not a person.

****

Lisa's car was in the driveway when he pulled into his usual spot. He wondered whose spot it would be in a year. Would she have found someone else to love in such a short time?

"She is a beautiful woman," he said to himself as he fell out of the truck. "Someone will snap her up in a minute."

"Who's a beautiful woman?" she asked, rounding the corner to gather him up into her embrace.

She smelled good.

He held tight to her and wouldn't let her pull away. "I love you," he said.

"I love you too, babe, but you're squeezing the life outta me."

He closed his eyes, willing the pain in his chest to go away. He released her and she grabbed his hand, pulling him across the expanse of the lawn and through the front door of their 1950s ranch house.

"How did the doctor go?" she asked, as she rounded the counter of the bar that separated their living room from their dining room.

"He went," he said, settling back in his favorite recliner. He wanted it to be normal for a little while longer, was that so bad?

He knew the moment the words escaped his mouth they would never be the same. Their lives together would be on a countdown and they would never know how long was left until the buzzer sounded. The thought of everything they are being torn asunder by one little word, one huge word, was too much for him to take.

They needed this moment of normalcy, even if she had no idea this would be their last.

"Tony," she said, bringing his drink over to where him. "How did it go?"

He opened his eyes, taking in her beauty. This instance was it. This was the last.

His heart broke.

He took the glass, taking a long slow sip as she perched on the ottoman beside his feet.

"You're scaring me," she said. "Is it bad?"

He lowered his glass. "It's bad," he said finally.

Tears began to build over the clear blue that was her eyes. "What did he say?" she asked, her voice a tremor.

"In some patients this is a long term illness that is treatable. In fact, seventy percent of those who detect it early can survive it." He really wished he'd detected it earlier.

"Tony," she sobbed.

"I'm sorry, honey," he said.

Placing his glass on the glass topped table beside the chair, he pulled her to him, holding her there while they both sobbed.

"I'm so sorry."

Happier

How do I get happier? Is that question even in the correct form?

Daphne stared at her computer screen, uncertain whether or not she could answer the question. Well, either of them. How could she get out of the funk that had been holding her down since the beginning of term? This was her final semester as an undergrad student and she was no closer to having an identity in her field of study than she had been in the beginning.

She closed her eyes, grinding her palms against her eyelids. This never helped. Why did she think that an answer could be squeezed from her subconscious?

"Hey, D," Goya, her roommate said from her side of the sparsely decorated room. What a pity this is what passes for an apartment in this town, she thought. Their living room/bedroom/kitchen/entertaining area was about the size of a motel room, and the bathroom they were forced to share with the other six people living on the floor was about the same size. She hated it here.

Hated it.

"Yeah?"

"I'm going out for a bit tonight. Do you mind leaving the door open for me?"

"Why? So I can be murdered in the middle of the night only to be discovered by you three days later when you actually make it back?"

She looked stunned for a moment, like she didn't know whether to laugh or be offended by her candor. "First, I will be back in the morning at the latest. I have an early class, so I can't be out all night." She moved to the mirror, her luscious lips in a full pout as she applied the soft pink lippy she always used. "Second, maybe it would do you a little good to get out. You stay in this room too much. It's making you grumpy."

"Goya, please stop talking to me." She raked her hands through the long tangled mass hanging from her head. "I have too much to do to be going out every night and doing who knows what with whomever you do it with."

Goya laughed. "You are far too young to be so bitter." She made a kissy face to the mirror and fluffed her black twenties bob to give it a little bit of body.

She fingered her own hair, wishing she could care what it looked like.

Her roommate turned to her. "Stand up."

"What?"

"Stand up."

"I thought you had somewhere to be. You don't want to be late, do you?"

"Nope. But I also can't go out and have a good time knowing that you are sitting here sulking. Again."

"What do you care?" she quipped, standing up as her roomie yanked on her arm. "You would have more space if I rotted away in here."

"Yes, but I wouldn't get to see your sour face anymore and then what would I do?"

Daphne laughed. "Whatev. Let's get this over with. I have a paper to write."

"And when is it due?" She asked as she pulled a brush through Daphne's hair. "Two weeks from now?"

"So what, I like to stay ahead. It helps if I get sick."

"No, you like to hide." Daphne closed her eyes, trying not to think about the torture her hair was being submitted to. Goya tugged, twisted, and shook it out. "Just like you've been hiding since..."

"Don't say it."

Goya whirled her around. Before she knew it she was being assaulted with a PONDS face cleansing wipe and then a barrage of different colors were being applied to her face. She knew it wouldn't do any good to struggle, so she stood in defeat awaiting the moment when she would be released.

"I guess I don't need to say it then," Goya said with a sigh. "That is admission enough for me. It just seems like you are a different person since... well, you know."

"I *am* a different person." She slumped. "I just need to focus on school. This is the last semester of our undergrad and then I will be moving on to a bigger school. I'm in the perfect place to concentrate right now. I don't have any complications getting in my way."

"Yeah, well I know someone that would *love* to be a complication in your life."

She chanced looking at her roomie. "Really?"

"Yup."

"Who?"

Goya grasped her by the shoulders, nudging her over to the full length mirror. "Not telling. It wouldn't do any good to, so I won't."

She turned Daphne around and suddenly the girl who'd been trying to hide form herself for months was standing face to face with her. Goya's lips pulled back in a soft smile.

"It's time to get past it, kiddo," she said, grabbing the leather coat she'd flung over her bed. "You loved and you lost. He was a jerk to end it the way he did, but you don't need to lose yourself because of it. It's time to pick yourself up and dust yourself off." She leaned in and kissed Daphne on the back of the head. "I'll be at the Pond if you want to join me," she said as she bounced out the door. "Lates!"

She surveyed the girl in the full length mirror. Goya had done wonders with the brown mass that hadn't seen a brush in weeks. It had scarcely seen the shower! She'd painted her eyes with amethyst and created a smoky look that smoldered, making her anger look almost sexy.

She laughed. Sexy. Yeah, right!

Her hair was in a bun and long tendrils fell over her shoulders and onto the old jersey t-shirt she hadn't washed in weeks. How often did you need to wash your night clothes anyway?

But still, her head was in stark contrast with the rest of her.

She went to the bureau on her side of the room and pulled out her favorite jeans and lavender sweater. Careful not to disrupt the perfect-ness of her hair she pulled the clean duds on and went back to face herself in the mirror.

She was different, that was for sure. Six months ago she had been happy. It had shown in her eyes, her mouth, and her body. She was in love and sure of her future. She knew what she wanted. Well, for the most part. She had never felt sure of her field of study, but he had always been there to cheer her on. It was his field of study too and they were going to work together and be happy.

Happy.

And then he had slid a note under her door that he was in love with Stacy Marquise. Her stomach clinched at the thought of her and what she had accomplished. She had managed to throw asunder a three year relationship with the man Daphne had been sure she would marry.

She shook her head.

Maybe Goya was right. Maybe.

But what if she did choose to go out tonight? They were always at the Pond, which was why she had decided to stop going. What if she gathered the courage to go out and meet up with people to have fun and then there they were?

Walking back over to her desk, she plopped down in the old wooden chair her father had suggested. He thought it would help her think better if she sat on something sturdy and "old world."

How do I get happier? Her computer screen asked her.

"I don't know," she said, her voice shaky. Then, stretching her arms out she typed, *Get out.* "Maybe."

She turned to the book lying beside her keyboard. She'd read it three weeks ago and had even written the paper for it, but she was contemplating a rewrite just because she didn't have anything else to do.

Didn't have anything else she *wanted* to do.

She closed the book and stood up. Grabbing her keys, she rushed out of the room before the feelings of uncertainty could stop her. She was all the way out the front door when she finally stopped to take a breath.

The campus was quiet, save for the stray kid here and there. In the quad she could see Jason Haynes, all glory and gloat, flirting with two freshmen. She often wondered if there was any end to his skeez. Judging by the looks of the conversation, his confidence and the two younger girls shy glances and giggles, it stretched farther than the imagination.

It all seemed foreign, her being out of the "house" on a Friday night all painted up and wearing the guise of normal. She didn't belong here anymore. But that didn't stop her legs from propelling her forward and toward the hang out she'd frequented with the man who'd broken her heart.

It was crowded. Not unusual for a Friday night. The main room was probably the size of a Waffle House, but the kitchen was separate here, so the room taken up by kitchen and counter tops in those establishments was filled with bistro tables, comfy chairs, and sofas.

She jumped at the sound of the door closing with a thud behind her. She didn't want to look up. She was too sure that all eyes would be on her and, worse, that they would be laughing, but when she managed a peek no one had even bothered to look her way.

Breathing deeply, she stepped into the chaos of the packed room, searching for Goya and her boyfriend of three months, Brandon. His orange hair shouldn't be that hard to spot.

"Daphne!" Moni Shars squealed, stepping up beside her. Moni was graduating with her and Goya, but the rumor was that she shouldn't be. She was model gorgeous with super short brown hair, a perfectly sculpted face, bright green eyes, and legs that went all the way up. It had been Moni that Daphne had been worried about initially and most certainly not Stacy. "It's been *so* long since I've seen you," she said, her voice as shrill as it ever had been. "I actually thought you quit," she cackled. "But Stacy told me that you were still lurking about!"

She managed a laugh, though her stomach was now twisting into knots. "Yeah," she said, her voice muffled by the sounds of those around her.

"I totally think you should come over and sit with us!" Moni said. "All the old gang is in the corner. I just came over to get another drink." She raised her hand to wave at the table in the far corner of the room.

"I really don't think..."

"Oh come on!" she said, grabbing Daphne's hand. She was having a great time at her expense and it was only serving to illustrate Daphne's earlier point to herself. She didn't belong here anymore. "Doolie is *dying* to see you!"

Doolie. She had given him that name, but by the third year of him having it neither could remember exactly how she'd come to call him that. His birth name was John, but she hadn't called him that since the time she'd run into him in the courtyard two months after their breakup.

She jerked her hand away and Moni looked at her as if she'd just been slapped.

"If *Doolie* wanted to see me so badly he knew where to find me." She straightened up, not wanting to appear pathetic in case John was looking. She'd been pathetic enough over the last half year. "It was lovely seeing you again, Moni, but I am meeting someone."

She laughed. "Who? Cause I heard you're all shriveled up."

She wanted punch her. Wanted to make her gut hurt as badly as her own was hurting, but instead she forced a laugh and walked away.

"Hey!" Goya said, throwing her arms around her roomie. "You're shaking, what's up?"

"Moni Shars."

"Ugh." Pulling her into another hug she whispered. "The guy beside Brandon is Nick. He's totally into you. Be nice."

Daphne smiled. "I promise." She stepped over to the extremely cute guy she remembered from Biology last spring. He was jock cute, something she didn't normally go for, with strawberry blond hair and the cutest dimples. She was more into nerdy guys. John was the biggest nerd she'd ever met. But Nick was.... adequate.

"Hey!" he said, standing so they would be on a level plain.

"Hey," she said. "I'm Daphne."

"Nick."

She smiled, then looked over to the corner Moni had motioned to. Sitting there was the biggest nerd she had ever seen. And he was still as cute as ever.

"You okay?" Nick asked.

She turned back to him and smiled. "I wonder if you would allow me to do something," she said over the roar of the music blaring around them.

"What's that?" he asked.

Without listening to the rational side of her mind she grabbed him, pressing her mouth to his. He tasted like beer and nachos, but that was okay. At least tonight it was.

"Wow," he said, when she pulled away. "So, how are you?"

"Happier," she said. "Definitely happier."

Used

It was an odd sight for the little town of Denten. The population of 1200 hadn't seen something of such spectacle for quite some time. Sally Masters said things like this were bound to reach Denten, but no one ever listened to Sally Masters. She was crazy. Or at least that is what little Louise Pastor had always heard.

On this day Louise was standing next to her father, her little girl hand fitting snugly into his massive daddy one, in her favorite Sunday dress. It was green and yellow with a bellowing skirt that stopped at her knees. It made her feel like the prettiest girl in the world. And today, even though it was Wednesday and she had school the very next day her daddy was letting her wear her favorite dress, and they were going to eat at her favorite restaurant because he had something to tell her.

But something had stopped them on their way to the little pizza shoppe Louise would eat every day if her parents would allow it. The strange, and out of character incident unfolding before her eyes, those of her father's, and a great many of the townspeople was mystifying, and from the looks on the faces of those surrounding her, they were just as surprised and ignorant of what was happening as she was.

Mr. Filbert, the nice man that lived two streets over from her, was in the middle of town square, his large shiny blue Buick parked haphazardly behind him. He looked like a madman with his pastel yellow shirt unbuttoned, the wind blowing it open now and then to expose a badly stained undershirt. In one hand he was holding a large gun, the wooden handle propped up on his hip and the long metal part towering above his balding head. In the other hand he was holding tight to the arm of a very inappropriately dressed Mrs. Filbert.

Louise's mother always made comments about how pretty Mrs. Filbert is, how slender she is, and how she's lucky she has never had children, cause she'd mess up her figure if she did. Louise had always found the last bit odd. Her mommy was just as pretty and she had a child.

Mrs. Filbert didn't look her usual pretty self on this day. Her yellow hair was normally very neat looking with giant waves that cascaded over her shoulders and to the middle of her back.

Louise had always wanted hair like that, but her hair was more red than blond and was so thin she couldn't even get it to stay curled! She hoped her hair would be pretty like Mrs. Filbert's when she grew up. But today her hair was full of knots and was sticking to her face in places. Her eyes looked black, like one of those silent performers she'd seen on the beach one time when they'd visited the carnival, with black lines that smeared half way down her cheek.

Mrs. Filbert struggled against her husband, trying desperately to get away from him. Louise wished Mr. Filbert would give her his shirt. She didn't think it was right to have her standing there in her lady underclothes. They were pretty blue lace.

And she certainly didn't think Mrs. Filbert should have to keep that big sign around her neck. She strained her eyes to read the words written in a deep red.

"Used," she read aloud.

Her daddy's grip tightened on hers.

"Alright!" Mr. Filbert was yelling. His face was red and puffy. Louise couldn't believe how different he looked today. He wasn't at all like she remembered him. "Lookey here, huney," he said, getting so close to Mrs. Filbert that she moved her head away. "We've gathered a crowd!"

"Ralph, please," Louise heard Mrs. Filbert say.

"Please, what, Helen?" He looked to his townspeople, all of them staring with a mixture of confusion, horror, and disgust.

Louise looked at her daddy. His expression was blank. She wanted to ask him what was going on, but his grip (still tight) told her she shouldn't.

"Please don't tell these fine people what kinda woman they've got living amongst them!" He sniffed her, shoving his nose deep into her throat. "I bet they can smell it on you! I couldn't." He looked down and Louise thought she saw sadness. "You know what she told me today, folks?" There wasn't a movement from the crowd. "She told me she is in *love*, but it's not with me. Do I know him, I asked. What do you think she said?" He cackled. "She said he lives in town!" He cackled again, but Louise didn't understand what was so funny.

How can a woman married to a man love someone else other than her family?

"So now I will give you the chance, Mister Mystery Man, to save her life." He held the gun up high. "If you don't save her the woman you *love* is gonna get a blast right to her noggin." He tapped the barrel against Mrs. Filbert's head.

No one moved. Louise may have even bargained that most people had stopped breathing. Would they really watch Mr. Filbert kill his wife?

"No takers?" Shifting, he suddenly held Mrs. Filbert by both arms and was parading her around, moving the 'used' sign to the side so that every inch of her was exposed.

Louise felt her stomach flop over and over. She was going to be sick. She turned to her daddy to ask him to leave, but he wasn't even paying attention to her. She tried to pull her hand away, thinking that if she could get away from his increasingly sweaty hand she might feel a little better, but his grip was too tight.

"You coward!" Mr. Filbert shouted to the unknown man in the crowd. "She's good enough to run around behind my back, but she's not good enough to stand up for?" He jerked her around to face him. "I would have stood up for you," he spat, and then he shoved her to the ground, sticking the end of the barrel to her forehead.

Mrs. Filbert sobbed, begging her husband not to kill her. "I'm sorry," she choked. "I'm sorry, Ralph."

"STOP!" Louise shouted, unable to watch any more of this horror unfold.

Mr. Filbert looked over at her, then to her father. She looked at her daddy. She thought she saw an understanding pass between the two and then her daddy looked away. He always stood up for what was right. She couldn't understand why he wouldn't stand up for it now.

Mr. Filbert smiled. "You want her!" he yelled. "She's yours now."

Mr. Filbert walked over to his Buick and jerked two bags from the back seat. He tossed them and they landed in front of his wife. "Don't you *ever* come near me again, Helen," he shouted. "You're disgusting."

With that he jumped into his car, slammed the door, and sped down main street. He wasn't even going back to his house.

Louise turned her attention back to Mrs. Filbert, surprised to find her staring in her direction. And then, as if a veil had been lifted Louise realized that Mrs. Filbert wasn't staring at her at all.

"Daddy," she whispered, but he had already let go.

Opposite

He wasn't at all the kind of man she was ordinarily attracted to. Thinking back over her forty years she could only think of one other like him, but even then she had been eager to change the one thing that had drawn her to him. Even before she had secured him as a partner she'd improved his appearance in her mind; trimmed his hair, put him in slacks and a polo, and thrown his old dirty ball cap out the window.

But not this one.

Last time she had needed her partner to be presentable in her circle. She'd needed her friends to think he was good enough for her, not once considering whether or not she was good enough for him.

At least that's what he surmised upon their separation.

That was almost twenty years ago. After that experience she had vowed to never go through that again, to never allow herself to become lost to someone that society would not deem her equal. She had been blissful in her ignorance, going blindly into a romance with the man that would become her husband. He'd been her equal. Well, her equal in the eyes of society. But when it was all said and done twelve years later her eyes had finally been opened.

Whoever said a degree makes one clever never suffered at the hands of love.

Now here she was again, standing at the precipice. Attraction was supposed to be a simple biological reaction. Or so she'd heard. But the moment he comes into sight she is propelled beyond that. It's still biological at the root, but it grows and spreads to every fiber of her being; every nerve ending sparks, the hair on the back of her neck perks up, her hands begin to shake, and a warm wave travels over the entirety of her body. It is as if she is opening, shedding her form to transcend to another plain of existence.

How does this happen?

She is a professor of fine arts and he works on air crafts. The thought of him working with his hands never fails to send another jolt through her. He's average height and built like the laborer he is, his only definition brought about by the back breaking work he's always had to do. His hands are large and calloused, but so gentle. He isn't hard in appearance, nor is he delicate. His smile is shy and secret, and his emerald eyes sparkle with devilish thoughts. His traditional views quite often clash with her own, creating a heat capable of consuming everything around. He is gruff and matter of fact.

He is her complete opposite.

Standing, she makes her way out of her home office and into the sunroom where he keeps his computer. As usual he is in the middle of some online card game.

Silently she crosses across the threshold, her bare feet a whisper on the deeply stained bamboo floor. Raising a shaking hand she runs her palm along the fine hair that attempts, naturally, to cover the balding spot on the back of his head. He catches her hand, as he always does, and she smiles.

Without a word he pulls her into his lap and she begins to feel her worldly fibers strain against their mortal confines.

Soup

The best thing about the cold is settling in for a nice steaming cup of soup, Wendi Collins thought as she brought the bowl of steaming liquid to her lips. Most people couldn't wait for it to get really cold so that they could have hot chocolate, but for her it had always been about the soup.

Her mother had called it an unnatural obsession with soup, but she called it comfort in a bowl and something that she could absolutely gorge on and it wouldn't make much different. She had often thought it must have come from that uneventful season when she'd developed the flu and her mother had spoon fed her chicken noodle soup every single day until she was able to get out of bed. Something had told her then that her mother had only taken the time to spoon feed her because she had nothing else to do.

But instead Wendi believed it came from the winters she'd spent with her grandmother in the Appalachian mountains. Nothing could beat settling into the large overstuffed sofa situated in front of the old wood stove with her grandmother. Just the two of them talking in the warmth of that little two bedroom house, with nice heaping bowls of vegetable soup. It was her grandmother's favorite.

Those had been the happiest times of her life, and they continued to be until the passing of her grandmother three years before.

Now there was Abby. She and Marcus were the only ones that had been there when her grandmother had passed. Abby, her best friend and sister of the soul variety, and Marcus; nice guy, tall and lanky with an adorable face and sweet disposition, but he hadn't been prepared for how much losing her grams would affect her.

Abby had been the only one willing to be by her side through the mood swings and alcohol. Even the drugs.

The road down to the bottom varies for every person, but she shifted her car into turbo and made it to the bottom six months after her grandmother was lowered into the ground.

Her mother had been the first to give up. Then her father. Her sometime-friends were out before she'd even really maneuvered onto the highway, but Marcus held in there for as long as he could. He stayed there for the descent and tried as hard as he could to pull her out, but she was stuck. No one was getting her out.

Abby had understood that.

Where Marcus had tried to guide her out, Abby had stood watch, allowing her to fall and make her mistakes, but at the same time making sure she didn't kill herself in the process. She'd told her it had been the hardest things she'd ever done. Wendi believed her.

She'd been clean now for three months, had a job again, though it was nothing near what her previous job had been, and inherited the house she'd spent so much of her life in. So many happy memories.

Now she was standing in the driveway, her hand still holding tight to the bright blue door of her Honda civic, unable to move. How could she walk through that front door again knowing that her Grandmother wouldn't be on the other side with a smile and an engulfing hug.

She bent over slightly, trying to catch her breath.

How could she go into a house that most certainly smelled like the woman she had loved more than life itself and not slide back into the hell that had been her life for more than two years.

"Come on, Wendi," Abby said, placing her hand over the one that refused to detach.

She looked at her friend, unable to blink away the wall of tears blurring her vision. She shook her head. "I can't," she said, her tone strained.

"You can," Abby said.

Wendi took a deep breath, detaching her hand from the door. Her legs became like jello and her feet like cement blocks. It was an odd feeling, but one that she understood more than not. For two years she'd run away from this feeling.

The dread of facing the truth.

Abby slid an arm around her waist, allowing her to rest her head on her shoulder. Abby had always been there, ready to take on the weight of the world for her. The closer they came to the large front porch the heavier her legs became. Her chairs were still there. Four rocking chairs, two situated on either side of the porch, and a two-seater swing. They'd spent many afternoons on this porch, laughing and talking. Her grandmother had known all her dreams.

She'd known everything.

They climbed the three stairs to the landing and she was face to face with the door. She touched the wreath her grandmother had hung out just two weeks before her heart gave out on her.

She hadn't even known.

"You okay?" Abby asked, tucking the dark waves that had escaped Wendi's bun behind her ears.

Wendi nodded.

Abby turned the nob, pushing the door open.

Wendi breathed in the woman she had loved more than anything else in her entire life and folded to the floor of the porch.

Abby was beside her, holding her close and smoothing her hair back. "It's okay," she soothed. "It's okay."

Wendi grabbed at her blouse, the pink one she'd given her a month ago for her birthday.

"Come on, Wendi, we've got to keep going."

"I can't," she sobbed.

Abby forced her to look up. "You can," she said, her tone desperate and stern all at the same time.

Wendi shook her head, but Abby held her gaze. She swallowed, pushing down the anxiety, acknowledging where the pain was coming from.

She nodded.

Abby helped her up and they continued into the tiny house that she now owned.

Once inside she looked around. It was immaculate, just like it had always been. But how? Her mother wouldn't have come here. She was still bitter that the house was left to a grandchild and not a child. Her grandmother had always said her children didn't need anything she had to offer, and she wouldn't bother leaving them anything because they had no use for her in life.

"How can they have any use for me in death?" she would ask.

Wendi had always laughed, but she had never believed that she would leave them nothing, aside from photographs.

It was all hers.

So who?

She looked to Abby. "Did you do this?"

"Not me." She held her hands up. "Go into the kitchen," she ordered.

Wendi took a deep breath and made her way through the living room, pausing at the door before pushing it open to enter the kitchen.

The smell hit her the moment the door cracked and she paused. Vegetable soup. She looked back at Abby, but she was standing in the living room, her arms crossed over her abdomen. She lifted a lithe arm and motioned for her to move inside.

Wendi pushed the door open all the way and stepped inside, her eyes shut tight, too scared to look at what was waiting there for her.

"Hey," the voice came across the room.

It was not a ghost. Not in the literal sense anyway.

Her eyes fluttered open and she was faced with the man she'd never expected to see again. He was standing in the center of her grandmother's kitchen. *Her* kitchen. In his hands he held two bowls. She smiled, despite the overwhelming emotions raging inside her.

"Soup?" he asked, his lips twitching in the most endearing nervous smile.

"It was you?" she said, accepting the bowl, her mind reeling from the realization settling in. "It was you."

The Rest of Her Life

Marjorie Hibert rolled over, her aging hand trailing over the silver hairs of her lovers chest. If anyone had asked her two years ago whether or not she would take a lover after the death of her beloved Jonas her only answer would have been "Not in a million years", but here she was lying in the bed of a man she'd never expected to love. "Benson," she said, stirring him from his half-sleep.

"Yes, Margie?"

"What will we tell everyone?"

He chuckled. It was all so easy for him. "We're in love. What else?"

She smiled. It had been so long since anyone had loved her. By the end of his illness the love she and Jonas felt for one another was not that of man and woman as much as it was that of companionship. "But my children won't understand. Especially Kelly. She still hasn't gotten over her father's passing."

Benson turned to face her, his long slender hand sliding through the mass of silver on her head. "Didn't they know you two hadn't felt real love for one another for quite some time?"

His question seemed odd to her. She shook her head. "No. You never tell your children things like that. We could have ruined their lives. Especially Kelly's. She depended on Jonas and I so much."

"Well, Kelly is twenty-five now. I think she can handle it."

She swiped at her cheeks. "Oh, Ben…"

"Look, Marjorie, if they don't like the fact that you're in love that's their fault. But you're sixty years old, hon, love only comes by so often."

She took his hand into hers and sighed. "You're right. I know you are. They should be happy for me. And it's been two years since Jonas passed. I'm just so scared."

"I'm right here with you, sugar," he said, nuzzling her neck. "I know how much your kids mean to you and I don't expect to compete with that. Wouldn't want to. But I am here for you. No matter what."

She kissed him, loving him just a bit more for being there. They'd been seeing one another for almost a year and his patience was wearing thin, but he never pushed for her to tell. Only nudged. It would be best for them both, she knew that, but that thought of upsetting her children was just too much to bear.

"I know you are," she said pulling away. "And I love you so much more for that."

****

Marjorie could hear her daughter banging around in the kitchen when she entered the Craftsman she'd shared with Jonas for their entire forty year marriage. It was too large now with just her staying there. Kelly came over often, but not quite enough to make it feel like the home it had once been. In her youth she'd imagined the two of them surrounded by grandchildren at this point, not her shacking up with Benson and poor Jonas being six feet under.

"Mom, is that you?" Kelly called from her place in the kitchen.

"Yes, it's me," she answered, hanging her coat in the hall closet before making her way back to meet her daughter.

"So," Kelly said, leaning her lithe frame against the counter, her coffee mug poised to drink. "Where were you last night?"

Marjorie stopped in the center of the doorway. Her heart began to pound. She didn't want to lie to her daughter, but telling the truth didn't seem like the best idea either. "I was with a friend," she said, crossing the kitchen to get her own cup of joe.

Her eyes took on a devilish grin. "Who?" she asked.

"No one you know," Marjorie said, grabbing a mug from the cabinet and filing it with coffee.

"Come on, Mom," Kelly teased. "I know you have a boyfriend. Who is it?"

"Kelly," She was going to deny it, still thinking it best to keep quiet than reveal the truth, but here was her chance. Kelly had, miraculously, opened the door for her to come clean and profess her love for the man who'd stolen her heart. She smiled. "His name is Benson Jacobs."

She looked thoughtful a moment and Marjorie knew that she was trying to place him. "Is he the doctor downtown?"

"No," she laughed. "Doctor Jacobs is only thirty-five. That's a little young for me."

Kelly laughed. "Well, what does he do?"

"He's a retired Navy officer."

"I'm happy for you, Mom," she said, wrapping her arms around the neck of her still-stunned mother. "I was wondering when you would start to get over Daddy." When she pulled away her lips were still pulled into a smile. "You thought I would flip out, didn't you?"

"To tell you the truth I did," Marjorie laughed.

Picking her mug up from where she'd placed it on the counter, Kelly dumped out the rest of its contents and laughed. "I'm a grown woman, mom, not some miserable thirteen year old. I wish you'd told me sooner. I can't imagine how hard it was to keep that secret." Her arms were around Marjorie once more. "I love you and I want you to be happy."

She didn't move right away after Kelly bounced out of the room for work. Truth be told, she didn't think she was capable of movement at that moment, but when she regained the ability to move she made her way across the kitchen and dialed Ben's number.

"I told Kelly," she said when he answered on the second ring. "And she is happy for me. For us!"

"This calls for a celebration." She was happy to hear his tone lighten. "I'll cook."

"Sounds good to me," she almost sang.

"I'll see you around eight then."

She hung up the phone and leaned back against the pale yellow wall of the kitchen. The house seemed to fall away and she was floating away on her little cloud of happiness and for the first time in six months she didn't feel guilty about it.

****

"Ben," Marjorie said as she stepped through the door of his seaside cottage. It was much smaller than her old Craftsman, but just the right size for the two of them. Placing her coat on the hook she made her way into the dining room on the right. "Ben, are you here?"

"In the kitchen! Have a seat. Everything's almost done!"

She surveyed the place settings spread out before her. Delicate china that she was sure had been a gift at his wedding. She thought about his wife, a woman she'd known in her youth. Ben didn't talk about her often and Marjorie knew it was because they hadn't had the best marriage. They'd married right out of high school due to their first child being born and had stayed married until three years ago when she had succumbed to cancer. Marjorie didn't pressure him to talk about her, figuring there would be plenty of time enough for that.

All that she wished for him was to be as close to his three children as she was to her two. Unfortunately, it would never be that easy for him. Especially not now that he'd told them about seeing her. She suspected that his patience in dealing with her came from the way his own daughter reacted to his moving on.

"Do you like it?" he asked, carrying in a large platter and two serving bowls. He looked like an old waiter in his black slacks and white button up.

She smiled. "I love it."

He leaned over, kissing her square on top of the head, then ruffled her hair. "Nothing is too good for my honey."

After dinner they settled into the old brown sofa situated in front of the fireplace in his living room sipping on a dark flavorful coffee he'd promised her she would love. She did. They sat quietly for a while, watching as the flames of the fire licked up toward the darkness of the chimney. It was a comfortable silence. Nothing expected. Nothing lingering. It was only the two of them in the dim light of his little living room. She couldn't have asked for anything more.

But then he gave it to her.

Lifting the cup from her hand and placing it on the table beside her he kneeled down in front of her.

"Ben, what…"

He pulled a small blue box out of his pocket and she caught her breath. "Marjorie, I have waited to have you for more than twenty years. Now I've got you and I never want to let you go. I want to love you until the day I no longer have breath in my body. Will you be my wife?"

She nodded, unable to form words. With a shaking hand she removed the engagement ring Jonas had placed on her hand so long ago, allowing Ben to replace it with the glittering solitaire he'd picked out just for her.

"I love you, Marge," he said. "Now and forever."

****

She sat in the overstuffed chair situated in front of her sofa and coffee table. Jonas had always given her free reign of the house decoration and had never questioned her when she'd spent money to redecorate. She fidgeted with the new ring on her finger as she watched her son pace back and forth between the sofa and cocktail table that had been in Jonas' family for more than sixty years. That had been is one stipulation with her decorating. She couldn't get rid of his mother's coffee table. There hadn't been a need to. It went quite well with her simple design.

"You're what?" Donald said once more, shoving his hand through the thick black mop on his head. He looked so much like his father.

"She's getting married, Donald," Kelly said. "Geez, no matter how many times she says it the root will be the same. She is *getting married.*" She emphasized the last part as if spelling it out for him.

"I heard her," he said, shooting his sister a look that could kill. "How could you even *think* of marriage? Dad hasn't even been dead that long!"

Marjorie opened her mouth to speak, but Kelly was right back up in her brother's face, her brown hair bobbing back and forth with each movement of her head. "Dad's been dead for two years, Donald! Mom and I have mourned and are *trying* to move on!"

"Will you let Mom talk?" He shouted, then turned his attentions to Marjorie. "Mom, how long have you known this guy?"

"More than twenty years," she answered. "He and his wife used to come over when you were both quite young."

He sat down, seeming to take into consideration that she'd known this man longer than a few months. He looked to the floor and then back to his mother. Marjorie was hopeful her eldest child was beginning to at least accept her impending marriage, but he was back up again glaring at her with anger in seconds. "Where is Dad's ring?"

"In my memory box," she said, covering her left hand. He began to pace again like a caged animal. Marjorie stood up, tired of the childish actions of this thirty-four year old man she'd given so much to. "My goodness, Donald, I expected this from Kelly, but not from you." She tried to reach out to him, but he held his hands up as if she were infected with some sort of communicable disease.

"Don't touch me," he almost shouted. "How can you do this?"

"Do what?" she asked, keeping her tone even and calm. "Be happy? Move on with my life? That's what your father would have done had our roles been reversed. I bet that would be okay, wouldn't it?"

"That's different."

"How? Because a man isn't supposed to be lonely, but a woman is?"

He lowered his head. "People are going to talk about you."

"Yes," she said. "They're going to say *look, Marjorie pulled herself together. Good for her!*"

"No," he said. "They're going to accuse you of not loving Dad enough to mourn him!"

"I can't mourn forever, Donald," she said, sitting back down. "I need companionship too."

He seemed to take that into consideration and, once again, she found herself hoping that he would relent and accept the changes in her life. "I have to go," he said, grabbing his coat from where he'd discarded it on the sofa.

"Let me walk you out," Marjorie said standing, but he shook his head.

"No, Mom. I'll be fine."

"Donald," she said, stopping him before he exited into the foyer. "I want you at my wedding. It's next month at the church. Will you come?"

He didn't answer.

When the door slammed Marjorie fell into her chair, tears spilling down her flushed cheeks. "What have I done?" she sobbed.

"He'll come to his senses, Momma," Kelly said, wrapping her up in a hug.

"He hates me."

"No, he doesn't," Kelly insisted. "He just needs time to think."

"Maybe I should just call it all off."

"Don't you dare!" She forced Marjorie to look up at her. "You are getting married to that wonderful man who loves you. You need to experience love. True love." She smiled at the look of shock on her mother's face. "It's a beautiful thing." She hugged her mother so tight Marjorie thought she might squeeze the life out of her. "Now, dry those tears. We've got a wedding to plan."

****

Majorie looked at her reflection, surprised that a sixty year old woman would look so beautiful in a wedding gown. She'd had her doubts about wearing white, but Kelly had assured her that it would be fine. She'd been pleased with the cut of the dress and her daughter had deemed it *very age appropriate*.

She touched the curled ends of her new bobbed haircut. This had been her idea. For so long she had been carrying around what remained of her old life in that shoulder length hair. When Jonas had been alive she hadn't had much time for her own upkeep and she'd continued that trend for a long while after his death. At first it had been because she hadn't known what to do with herself, and then it had simply become a matter of ignoring what she didn't like.

That old Marjorie was gone now. She smoothed an errant strand of silver and smiled at the woman standing before her.

"You look beautiful," Kelly said from the door.

Marjorie smiled. "Do you think I'm gussied up enough?"

"The only thing missing is your something blue, I think," Kelly said, holding out an old blue broach that her grandmother had worn on her wedding day.

"Where did you get this?" Marjorie asked as her daughter pinned it at the base of her throat.

"From your jewelry box. I know grandma wore it at her wedding and you did when you married Dad. I thought you might want to wear it to this one too."

"Marjorie smiled. "Thank you, sweetie."

Kelly turned her to face the mirror again. "Perfect," she whispered.

Marjorie blinked away the tears blurring her vision. "Have you seen Donald?"

"No." She frowned. "I'm sorry." Situating the veil on her mother's head she said, "Do you want me to walk you down the aisle?"

She shook her head. "No, honey, that's okay."

Kelly wiped the tears that had fallen from her mother's eyes, wrapping her up in a loving embrace. "Don't cry, Mom, he'll come around."

"I know, honey. I know." She held tight to her daughter. "Let's go. The man of my dreams is waiting."

She'd never felt the kind of heartbreak and elation she was experiencing at that moment. If Donald could have met Benson she had little doubt that he would like him very much. He had that sort of personality that he could charm even the hardest of people. Not that Donald was hard. Just stubborn like his father.

Kelly held her mother's arm and Marjorie knew that she was worried about her. Why wouldn't she be? She'd managed to hold everything together while preparing for the wedding, but only because she had believed that Donald's love for her would bring him to the church, regardless of his feelings for the wedding.

But as they neared the chapel she began to lose every ounce of hope she'd had left.

"Hey, Mom," he said from behind them just as she braced herself to enter the chapel alone.

She turned, stunned to see Donald standing there in his rented tux. She knew it was rented because he'd always hated them. Just like Jonas.

"Am I too late?"

She smiled through her tears. "No, honey," she said. "You're not too late."

Kelly smiled at her brother, then kissed Marjorie and headed down the aisle to stand with the other bridesmaids.

Marjorie laced her arm through the arm offered by her son. "I'm glad you came," she whispered as they began to walk to the wedding march.

"Me too."

****

"It turned out to be the perfect day, didn't it?" Ben said as they lay wrapped in one another's arms.

"It did," Marjorie answered. "I was so happy Donald showed up, but it was the shock of my life."

"Oh yeah?"

"Yes, sir. He's just like Jonas and those men do not change their minds easily. In fact, it would have taken Jonas years to warm up to you. I mean, if he and Donald switched places."

He laughed.

She looked up at him. "So that makes me wonder how you did it."

"What? You think I had something to do with it?"

"It's the only reason he would have shown up today."

He smiled. "Maybe he just realized your happiness was the most important thing."

"Sure. And did you see the weather report tonight? Seems like hell just froze right over."

He cackled and she couldn't help but laugh too. "Okay, I admit it. I paid him a visit a few days ago. I knew you couldn't bear getting married without him. It was a long shot, but I took a chance." He raised her face to look at him. "I told you, honey, I am here for you. No matter what."

She kissed him, happiness engulfing her. She realized that Kelly had been right that day in her kitchen. True love was wonderful, and for the first time she knew that. She snuggled closer to her husband, happy that she would have him and his love for the rest of her life.

Turn the page to read *Promises*.
Just in case you missed it in
Second Chances; and other tales of love...

Promises

Married. Just saying the word was like being beaten with a mace. How could he be getting married?

The day had begun so simply; wake up, get the kids ready for school and John ready for work, make eggs, shove everyone out the door, collect the mail, and open the overly optimistic yellow envelope that had the audacity to announce the blasphemous event.

How dare he!

With the envelope in slivers on the cherry-stained floor John and I had picked out the year before, I picked up the phone and dialed the only number I knew to dial.

"Can you believe this?" I screamed at Dakota, my best friend of forever. "Can you? Did you get one too?"

"Of course I did," she said, her tone unaffected.

"Well?"

"Well what, Janey?"

"Can you believe it?" I was pacing my dining room, going back and forth from the window that looked out onto our sleepy street to the super-happy invitation that had obviously been picked out by a moron. "I can't believe it! Can you believe it?"

"It was bound to happen at some point," was all she offered.

I could imagine her piddling around her tiny two-bedroom apartment, scooping up toy cars left out by her six-year-old son, and wads of paper courtesy of her husband.

"What did you think?" she was saying. "He would pine over you for the rest of his life?"

I picked up the card, my eyes roaming over the swirling letters that announced the nuptials of two people who shouldn't be together. "I think I'm going to vomit," I muttered.

Dakota laughed, a loud quip meant to shake me out of my funk. Apparently she had no idea just how deep it went.

"What?" I snipped.

"Are we really going to do this again?" she asked. After a pause from my end she sighed.

I didn't need her to tell me how pathetic I was being. I would have to be a complete moron not to realize that ten years after a breakup I shouldn't still be stalker-girl or miss obsess-much, but that didn't stop it from being so.

"Janey, why do you keep doing this to yourself?"

"I don't know," I lied.

Of course it was a lie. I knew exactly why I kept going on and on about him. Why I couldn't let him go. At least I thought I did. It all seems to get so muddled where Ryan Foust is concerned.

"You've got John," she said.

"I know," my lips said, but my mind couldn't keep from screaming at her; thanks for making me feel worse!

My story was supposed to be like Jane Austen's *Persuasion*. We were supposed to be apart for a while, but eventually we would fulfill fate and be together. We had a forever thing. Or so I thought.

"I don't know what's going on with me!" I shouted. "Every time I think I'm past him I find out I'm not!"

"So what now? Are you going to the wedding?"

"Don't we have to?"

"No!" she screeched. "This is *so* not good for you!"

"John might want to go," I tried.

She laughed. I could always count on her to call me on my bullshit. "Yeah sure!" she cackled. "John and Ryan are *such* great friends!"

"Dakota,"

She continued to laugh, that puttering half-laugh a person gives when they're slowing down.

"I have to go," I said.

"I know," was her saddened reply.

~*~*~ The Wedding ~*~*~

I had worn my best dress, a brown halter that dropped just below the knee. It was tasteful, but at the same time it was hopeful. My hair was twisted within an inch of its life on the top of my head, with my freshly shorn bangs swept to the side for a softening effect, and just a whisper of make-up. John had been sure to rave about me before I stepped out the door. Dakota had decided to out-fabulous me with a light purple summer dress and a loose braid that stretched from her shoulders to the small of her back. She loved weddings and today was no exception.

The groom and bride were in their respective chambers putting on their final touches, while their guests milled around the sanctuary chatting with acquaintances. There were more fond memories being shared that I could bear, so I took leave of the room.

My memories of Ryan involved his lopsided grin, and the way the world lit up when those blue eyes would turn on me with an insurmountable amount of love, or his laugh- deep and goofy- late at night when he shouldn't have been in my room. His lips had burned an impression on every inch of body they had touched, burning years later with the remembrance. He had the kind of kiss that was deep and devouring, and each time our lips met I felt sure he would swallow me and I would become part of that fiery being. Then there were the memories of his hands, so strong and so tender, the way they could ease all tensions or awaken my senses; or the hours I could spend just tracing every ridge of them, the calloused fingers that knotted at the knuckles and the smooth padding of the hand. How could I share those stories with anyone other than myself? Or the groom?

I can't say why I thought at that moment, as I stood in the foyer of the Baptist church, that it would be a good idea to go to him, but I did. And so I sought him out, that copper-haired boy who had broken my heart.

I stopped briefly by the room I found to be the bride's, wishing that I could burst in and rip every strand of brown hair from her optimistic head. I wanted her to hurt just like I was hurting. How dare she have the happiness that should have been mine? Instead I listened to her go on and on about how great it was that she was going to be Mrs. Ryan Foust. Pushing away from the door I continued down the hall, falling back a little when the door opened and Ryan's brother stepped out.

"You look great, man," he said. "Now hurry the hell up!" The laugh that flowed out into the hall was unmistakable, one that reminded me of afternoons huddled up together on a two-seater sofa, my finger tracing the tattoo his friend had given him the week before.

After I was sure he had gone I stepped up to the door and gave three quick taps. Part of me hoped he wouldn't answer, that he would be too preoccupied with the task at hand. But he did, and my breath caught at the sight of him standing full inside the door, still tall and lanky- except for the workingman muscles- in his tuxedo, that copper hair trimmed just above the collar, and those eyes...

"Janey?"

"H-hi, Ryan."

"What are you doing here?"

"I was invited!" That was me, defensive to a fault.

"I know. Deirdre told me she was sending you one. I meant why are you back here?"

"Oh. I hoped we could, um, talk."

When I saw the uncertainty in those pools that had once been so adoring I wanted to sob. When had it changed? When had they forgotten me?

"Did anyone see you come here?"

"You mean Ursula?"

"Her name is Kim," he said with that lopsided grin.

"I know," I pouted. "Ursula is just the ugliest name I could think of."

He gave a sort of half-laugh. "Come inside. I need to get finished."

When the door was closed and he was back in front of the mirror I could feel it coming, the **why** that was bound to come out in this conversation.

"So, what's up?" I asked, taking a seat on the closest piece of furniture, an old leather ottoman. He raised an eyebrow and I laughed. "Right."

"What about you?" he asked. "How's John?"

"Fine. Fine." I shifted on the ottoman, wishing that I could disappear into its dark leather. "He sends his apologies. He had some pressing business."

He laughed. "Yeah right."

Why? My mind screamed as he adjusted his seams and cummerbund. I stood, going to the bookshelf that lined the left wall, not surprised to find mostly religious texts.

"It's a nice turnout," I offered.

"You think so?"

He was right behind me. When had he moved so close? This wasn't something I could handle! He was not the person I could be so close to. Not now. I feigned interest in a book by the window across the room and made my way over.

"Do you remember getting a message from me two years ago?" I asked, secure in the distance between us. "I asked you to call me back and maybe we could hang."

"Yes, I remember." He walked back to the mirror pretending to fidget with his hair. "I thought it might be weird."

"It actually would have helped me a lot," I said, finding the courage to face him.

"How?" he asked.

"I was trying to work through some issues. I thought talking to you would help me before I made some really stupid mistakes."

"How?"

"I don't know. Maybe I just wanted to see you, to know that you still… thought of me." I shook my head. "For so many years we had this… *thing* between us. I rested easy in the knowledge that you still cared for me." I turned back to the window. "But I got the message. Loud and clear."

"What message?"

I whirled around, suddenly infuriated by his lack of devotion to our conversation.

"You never called, Ryan, what other message *would* I get?"

He made a move, as if he would turn back to the mirror, but stopped midway and faced me once more. "Janey,"

"I just wanted to know if you cared, Ryan," I interrupted, not allowing him a moment to dissolve my resolution. "If you ever *really* cared at all, but it was obvious that you didn't." I sat down. "It sounds silly, but that actually helped for a while."

I was a jumble of nerves. Unable to sit still I stood up again, moving closer to my only friend in that room, the window that shown bright the perfect day before us. I wouldn't be able to stave off my tears for long. I knew that, and yet I stayed.

"I thought that you had never cared for me and, somehow, that had provided me with enough courage to let go. For a while."

"I never intended for you to think that," he said, crossing the room.

"Really?" I asked, my voice a little too shrill for my own liking. "Then what is this?"

"What is what?"

"This!" I motioned to his tux and the room surrounding us. "Is this you *caring*?"

"What do you mean?" he asked.

"If you care about me how can you do this?"

"Janey, you're married."

"Yeah. And?"

"Are you saying that I am supposed to remain single and pine for you for the rest of my life?"

I shook my head, the loose bun flopping up and then down.

"Why?"

His look of contempt grabbed me. Before I knew it I was standing inches away from him, my face turned up toward his. My heart was pounding, and I swear I could actually *feel* my blood beginning to boil.

"Because you broke my heart!"

He stepped back as if my words had physically struck him.

"You were the **only** one for me and I knew that the *second* I set eyes on you! I waited a year to be with you and you broke my heart after three months! We were supposed to be forever and you shit all over me!" I swiped at my eyes, hating that I was crying over him again. "You promised to love me!"

"Janey,"

"I never stopped. I have loved you from the moment you pushed off that brick building and I am *so* stupid that I am sure to love you for the rest of my pathetic life!"

It was like an out of body experience, me screaming at him, my hair flying around my face- which I was sure had turned the color of a wildfire- and Ryan standing there with a look I hadn't ever seen before on his face.

"You want to know the worst part, Ryan?" I pulled the invitation out of my handbag, pushing it into his face. "When this came in the mail all I could think was *what's wrong with me? Why couldn't he marry* **me?**"

Sadness and- possibly imagined- tears clouded his eyes. But where I once would have seen loving feelings of regret I now saw mocking. I had loved this man for more than ten years and he was confirming how pathetic I had become. It should have stopped the moment he uttered the words, *"my friend's say it's them or you. I choose them."* Those three words that had shattered my sense of self should have been enough to make me dislike him, but instead I had harbored these intense feelings for him. Now he would get married and I would no longer exist, not even in the smallest corner of his heart.

"Forget it," I said, swaying a little from the downturn my roller coaster was taking. "I should have known." I pressed the invitation to his chest. "Enjoy your happiness," I sobbed, unable to think of anything else to say.

Dakota was outside the room, along with Kim and half the wedding party. I let the door open wide as I stepped out and fell into Dakota's outstretched arms, much like a drunk who has to be *helped* to their car at closing.

"What's going on?" Kim asked. She looked first to Ryan and then to the mess that I had become. "Ryan?" She looked almost comical standing there with half her empire braid out, that mousy brown hair looking more like a fried mess.

I looked back at Ryan and then to his ladylove. I wanted her to know that the man she was about to pledge the remainder of her life to was a liar and a promise-breaker, but at the same time I wanted to throw myself into his arms and beg him to love me.

Instead I looked to Ryan's sister, whose mouth was twisted up in a frightful smile. She had never liked me. I suspected that was why she had invited me, to see me die over and over again as the two lovers recited their vows. "I'm sorry," I said. "But I must decline your gracious invitation."

Dakota was proud, but I couldn't help feeling more empty than I ever had.

"I've got to change things," I sobbed as she dumped me into her Honda civic. "I can't do this anymore."

"It'll be okay," she soothed.

And I hoped she was right.

~*~*~ 1 Year Later ~*~*~

I slid my phone into the precious little hobo bag that had called from the rack at my favorite thrift store and stood up from the little bistro table at the finest little café in town. It was new, but the salad hadn't been half bad. I turned, eager to get going, completely unprepared for the collision between myself and the man who would torment me for the rest of my life.

"I'm so sor…" My voice caught for a moment when I realized just who I was staring at. It was devastating how handsome he always managed to be. "Ryan?"

"Janey, how are you?"

"Fine." I threw my bag up onto my shoulder, tucking my hair, a habit I'd always had. "You?"

"Good."

I tried to smile, although this chance meeting felt awkward as hell. Here is the man whose wedding I had essentially crashed with my unresolved issues. All I wanted to do was melt into nothing.

"How's John?" he asked, his voice cracking in the adorable way it always had.

"Fine," I said, not wanting to tell him John and I had separated a few months before. "How's Kim?"

"Fine." He shifted, running those hands over his jeans. As I watched them slide down and then back up the dark material that familiar ache began to awaken.

"Well," I said almost in a panic. "I gotta go. It was really great seeing you."

"Janey," he said, stopping me mid-sprint.

I turned around, pasting a stupid smile on my face. One look at those eyes and the darkness that they held is all it would take to undo a year of hard work. What would I interpret this time? Would I sense that he wanted to tell me how much he had always loved me? How much he still loved me?

I held my hand up, terrified for him to speak.

"Please," I said. "I can't." I smiled, blinking back the wall of tears beginning to blur my vision.

He nodded, and I walked away hoping- for my sake- to never see him again.

About the Author

Sayword Eller lives in central North Carolina with her husband of seventeen years and their three children. She is currently working to complete her MFA in History at High Point University and is still dedicated to the notion of love and every trifle that comes with it! Her first novel, SHADOWS, is slated for release in 2013.

Follow Sayword on:

www.twitter.com/prompting365

www.goodreads.com/saywordeller

www.authorsden.com/saywordbeller

www.prompting365.com